"You're such a wild...
appreciation

He couldn't have been more surprised. Before he could blink, Reilly had essentially ripped off his clothes, pulled her T-shirt over her head and shimmied out of her decadent jean cutoffs. Then she'd pushed him to the couch and straddled him, her lips full and pouty and her body primed and more than ready.

Now her hazel eyes twinkled, amusement and a hint of a challenge in them. "I'm a woman into extremes. When I do something, I go all the way." She wore a determined expression. "What's the matter, Ben? Afraid you can't handle a woman like me?"

This Reilly was so different from the self-conscious woman he was coming to know that he had to take another look to make sure it was the same person.

And the contrast turned him on to no end.

"Not the case at all, Reilly. I just want to know where the fire is."

She curved her fingers around his wrist, then tugged his hand down until his fingers rested against the front of her panties. She grinned wickedly. "Right here."

Dear Reader,

Sugar 'n spice and everything naughty literally applies to the second heroine in our KISS & TELL miniseries. Not only does Reilly Chudowski own a pastry shop named Sugar 'n Spice, but the treats she offers to Ben Kane are impossible for him to resist!

Only a woman who spent her childhood known as Chubby Chuddy would grow up to own a sweets shop…and be stupid enough to date L.A. restaurateur Benjamin Kane, a man renowned for his good looks and never-ending series of model girlfriends. But oh, how he feeds Reilly's growing appetites on every level. Only, when push comes to shove, can Ben convince her that there is life for them beyond dessert?

We hope you enjoy Reilly and Ben's delicious journey to sexily-ever-after! We'd love to hear what you think. Write to us at P.O. Box 12271, Toledo, OH 43612 (we'll respond with a signed bookplate, newsletter and bookmark), or visit us on the Web at www.BlazeAuthors.com and www.toricarrington.com for fun drawings.

Here's wishing you love, romance and hot reading!

Lori & Tony Karayianni
aka Tori Carrington

Books by Tori Carrington

FLAVOR OF
THE MONTH

Tori Carrington

HARLEQUIN®

TORONTO • NEW YORK • LONDON
AMSTERDAM • PARIS • SYDNEY • HAMBURG
STOCKHOLM • ATHENS • TOKYO • MILAN • MADRID
PRAGUE • WARSAW • BUDAPEST • AUCKLAND

If you purchased this book without a cover you should be aware
that this book is stolen property. It was reported as "unsold and
destroyed" to the publisher, and neither the author nor the
publisher has received any payment for this "stripped book."

We warmly dedicate this book to our niece Elena:
One word frees us of all the weight and pain of life:
that word is love.
—Sophocles
May you and Pantelis have love, always.

ISBN 0-373-79113-5

FLAVOR OF THE MONTH

Copyright © 2003 by Lori & Tony Karayianni.

All rights reserved. Except for use in any review, the reproduction or
utilization of this work in whole or in part in any form by any electronic,
mechanical or other means, now known or hereafter invented, including
xerography, photocopying and recording, or in any information storage
or retrieval system, is forbidden without the written permission of the
publisher, Harlequin Enterprises Limited, 225 Duncan Mill Road,
Don Mills, Ontario, M3B 3K9, Canada.

All characters in this book have no existence outside the imagination of
the author and have no relation whatsoever to anyone bearing the same
name or names. They are not even distantly inspired by any individual
known or unknown to the author, and all incidents are pure invention.

This edition published by arrangement with Harlequin Books S.A.

® and TM are trademarks of the publisher. Trademarks indicated with
® are registered in the United States Patent and Trademark Office, the
Canadian Trade Marks Office and in other countries.

Visit us at www.eHarlequin.com

Printed in U.S.A.

1

Hollywood Confidential—October 13, 2003

"…if you want this reporter's informed opinion, the crème de la crème of Hollywood eateries are Benardo's Hideaway and Sugar 'n' Spice. If the owners of these two delectable hot spots were to combine their talents, we'd all be in for a treat…."

REILLY CHUDOWSKI read and reread the piece in the daily paper her best friend, Layla, had left behind, gob-smacked by the unsolicited rave from the popular L.A. reporter. She sat back in the bar-style chair in her favorite corner of Sugar 'n' Spice and glanced out the floor-to-ceiling windows onto Wilshire Boulevard, taking in the autumn sunrise and the cars cruising by. A deep breath filled her nose with the smell of yeasty sweet rolls baking and coffee brewing and a touch of cinnamon from yesterday's cookies. Who would have guessed she'd be where she was now? Six months ago, she'd finally used the small amount of money her grandmother had left her and opened the doors to the pastry shop. Now, not only was she operating in the black, she was beginning to make a tidy profit. And with coverage like the *Hollywood Confidential* had just given her, things would likely get even better.

Yes, all was definitely right with the world....

Her smile slipped. Okay, maybe there was one little blemish. Her name had been linked with that of the owner of Benardo's Hideaway, Ben Kane. She didn't make a habit of buying the Hollywood hot sheets herself, but between her customers and her friends Layla and Mallory leaving the papers behind, she was kept pretty well informed when it came to L.A. social happenings and people of interest. Suffice it to say that dark-haired, sexy Ben Kane had enjoyed being the Hollywood Hunk of the Month for the past two years running. And while the *Confidential* reporter had likely met *him*, she probably had no idea who Reilly was, even though she'd obviously been in the shop. Because if she had, she'd never have linked Reilly and Ben Kane together in print, or in any other manner. Simply because people didn't come any more different than her and Ben Kane.

He was the captain of the football team and she was the fat girl in the back of the class.

He was the star and she was the extra with no lines.

He was the president and she was the disposable intern.

She lived in the cramped apartment over her shop and her only mode of transportation was a white ten-year-old minivan with the shop's logo painted on it. He likely had a sprawling mansion in the Hollywood Hills and drove a Ferrari.

Reilly absently folded the paper, the pad of her thumb catching on the edge.

"Ow." She shook her hand then stuck her thumb into her mouth. The cowbell above the front door clanged. She turned to find one of her morning steadies squinting against the change in light.

She pulled her thumb from her mouth. "Morning, Johnnie."

"And an awesome morning it is, too," Johnnie aka Johnnie Thunder said, just like he did every morning.

Reilly wondered if she was the only one who didn't operate under an alias in the greater L.A. area. She pushed from the stool, finding it amazing that she had steady customers. She took in Johnnie's limp, shoulder-length brown hair, his thickset torso bearing a pea-green T-shirt with a white logo of some kind on it peeking from the open flaps of his thriftshop army jacket. Worn jeans and tennis shoes finished off the effect of urban unchic. On a teen it might have been okay. But Johnnie had to be in his thirties.

"Can I interest you in a cream puff this morning?" she asked, scooting behind the counter where her eighteen-year-old niece, Tina, was stocking the display.

"No. I'll take a sweet roll and a small coffee."

"In other words, the usual?"

"Yeah."

Instead of immediately heading for his spot as he usually did after receiving his tray of items, Johnnie lingered awkwardly at the counter.

Reilly blinked at him as she rearranged the rolls for maximum effect. "Is there something more you wanted, Johnnie?"

Was it possible for a man his age to blush that deeply? Yes, she realized, it was.

"I was just wondering," he said. "I have tickets for this great music festival this weekend and I was thinking maybe you and me…well, if you wanted to go with me…"

She smiled at him, genuinely flattered at the attention, even if unwanted. "Thanks for thinking of me, Johnnie, but right now Sugar 'n' Spice is the whole of my professional and personal life. And it probably will be for the foreseeable future."

"Oh. Okay." He showed her the thin notebook computer tucked under his arm. "Mind if I hook up, then?"

"Actually, I'd probably tell anyone else who dared to sit there to get lost." She took in his half grin. "The spot's all yours."

He nodded, his stringy hair momentarily hiding his ferretlike features as he headed with his order for the table in the opposite corner that featured an electrical outlet and a cable modem hookup. She'd thought offering the service would attract more people of Johnnie's type, but so far he was the only one who logged on regularly. She wasn't all that clear what he did, but she was pretty sure Johnnie Thunder was his Internet name.

Her niece finished up then stacked an empty tray near the door to the kitchen. She shrugged out of her apron. "I've got to get to my nine o'clock."

"What's on tap this morning? Psych?" Reilly asked.

"Social Sciences." Tina—short for Constantina, and shorter yet for Constantina Kalopapodopoulos— blew dark brown bangs out of her darker eyes. She usually made it into the shop for an hour or two each day to help out and make deliveries, depending on her class schedule.

"You don't sound very happy about it."

Tina slanted a gaze at her. "Trying to juggle a full course load at UCLA while working two part-time jobs isn't a picnic, Aunt Rei."

"Well, if your motivation for wanting a degree in psychology was more than just about figuring out your dysfunctional family, maybe it wouldn't seem so tough." She rounded the counter again. "Besides, you forget that I've been there. The juggling part, I mean."

"Yeah, but that was at least…forever ago. Things have changed since then."

"Since four years ago?"

Tina rolled her eyes, looking more like her Greek-American father than her Polish mother—who was Reilly's sister—with every day that passed. "Whatever."

Reilly put a couple of cream puffs into a bag as Tina grabbed her backpack and jacket. She held out the bag as the eighteen-year-old passed.

Tina paused, her pretty face looking a little less harried. "Thanks."

"Is Efi stopping by to help out tonight?"

Efi was Reilly's secret favorite out of her nieces and nephews. She was Tina's younger sister and much hated by the older girl. At fifteen-going-on-forty, Efi reminded Reilly of what she'd been like herself growing up. Not a day went by that Efi didn't beg Reilly to hire her on full-time, though what she really wanted was to be a partner. But the only time Reilly gave in and let her help was when she had a large order to fill. And the catering gig for a charity event that weekend definitely qualified as a large order. More specifically, five thousand tiny éclairs.

"Yeah, she'll be here." Tina hurried for the door.

"Give 'em hell, kid!" Reilly called out after her.

While she couldn't see Tina's expression, she was pretty sure it involved an eye roll and a grimace.

Reilly shook her head as she picked up the empty baking trays and headed for the kitchen. The telephone on the wall next to the swinging door rang. She freed one of her hands and plucked it up. "Sugar 'n' Spice."

"And everything *very* nice," a familiar female voice said. "Have you gotten a load of this morning's *Confidential?*"

A documentary producer and one of her three best

friends, Mallory Woodruff rarely got excited about anything, so her enthusiasm warmed Reilly even further. "Why, yes, as a matter of fact, Layla brought by a copy earlier."

"Earlier? What time is it? Oh."

It was just after eight-thirty. Which made it much too early for Mallory although Reilly had been up since four-thirty getting ready to open her doors at six. When she'd first opened the shop, she'd posted her hours as seven. But that hadn't stopped at least a dozen or so people from knocking on her glass door with their car keys, their noses practically pressed against the window as they eyed where she was stocking the display cabinet. So she'd moved back the opening time. Which meant she also had to get up an hour earlier. But, hey, one didn't get mentioned in *Hollywood Confidential* by slacking off.

She caught herself smiling in the same goofy way she had been all morning.

"I think you should blow up the mention and post it in your front window," Mallory was saying.

"Too tacky."

"Well, frame it, *then* hang it in your window."

Reilly looked at the wall behind the counter. Maybe that wasn't such a bad idea. She could put it next to where she displayed in a frame the first dollar the shop had made and where her business license hung.

The front door opened, letting in another customer. Reilly looked in his direction. Another man. It was a given that the majority of her customers were female, aside from the men who stopped for coffee before eight. After eight, men were pretty scarce.

The expensive shine of rich leather shoes caught her attention first. Then her gaze moved up crisply ironed tan slacks, a belt that matched the shoes and up over a crisp brown-and-white striped shirt rolled up to reveal wrists peppered with dark hair. Mmm…if the rest of him matched what she'd seen so far…

Ever hopeful, she looked up into the handsomely familiar face that bore a passing resemblance to Tom Cruise.

She nearly dropped the phone.

Reilly swung away so she was facing the wall. Deciding that wasn't enough, she ducked through the swinging door leading to the kitchen, dropping the empty trays she held as she went.

She cringed at the earsplitting clanging that echoed through the kitchen and, undoubtedly, the rest of the shop.

"What was that?" Mallory asked as Reilly could do little more than stare at the noisy trays lying askew at her feet.

"You'll never believe who just walked in here."

"Are you whispering? You're whispering. So it must mean it's a star."

Reilly waved her hand as she restlessly paced one way then the other. "No, he's not a star."

"At least we've established it's a he."

"I mean, he's not a star in the conventional sense."

She caught her bottom lip briefly between her teeth and peeked out the round door window to find the man in question wearing an amused closed-mouth smile as he considered the goodies displayed behind the counter. He turned his head in her direction and she ducked out of the way again and flattened herself against the wall.

"Well, for God's sake, Reilly, who is it?"

She cupped her hand over her mouth and the receiver, "None other than Ben Kane himself."

Mallory's sigh filled her ear. "Here I was ready to ask you to get Russell Crowe's cell phone number for me. Ben Kane? He's just a restaurant owner. And why are you whispering anyway?"

Why *was* she whispering? She was in the kitchen. In her kitchen, in her shop, and there was certainly no one around to notice her, much less overhear her.

"I don't know," she admitted. "Maybe it's the piece."

"What, mentioning you and Kane in the same sentence?"

That didn't sound quite right, either. "Yeah."

"I think you need a nap."

Reilly dared another peek through the window to find Ben Kane staring pointedly at his watch.

"Oh, God, he's expecting service."

Mallory's throaty laugh filled her ear. "Of course, he is, silly. He's in a shop that sells stuff. Which means he's probably interested in buying some of that stuff." Reilly rolled her own eyes. "Now go sell him some of that stuff so, you know, you can make some more of that green stuff.''

"Very funny.''

"I am, aren't I? Oh, and Reilly?''

"Lord forbid I ask, but what?''

"Triple your prices. He can afford it.''

"I can't do that!''

"You don't have your prices displayed, right?''

No, she didn't. She figured her biggest sales point was her baking skills and display case.

"It wouldn't be right.''

Mallory sighed. "Fine, then. Be a good girl.''

God, how she hated being called that.

"I'll call you later,'' Mall said. "You know, after you've served Mr. Hot-Pants Kane and after I get back from scouting that shoot site.''

"Okay.'' Reilly told her friend goodbye then turned to hang up the phone. Only the base for the phone was on the other side of the door.

She closed her eyes wondering just how juvenile she looked. Even her fifteen-year-old niece, Efi, would probably shake her head in shame.

BEN KANE watched as the door to what he guessed was the kitchen opened a few inches. But rather than a person appearing, a slender hand snaked out holding a corded telephone receiver, blindly trying to hanging it up on the base.

He rubbed his chin. Odd. If he didn't know better, he'd think the girl who'd disappeared into the kitchen upon his arrival was trying to avoid him. But that didn't make any sense, because this was his first time inside the Art Deco-Style shop with its black and white floor tiles and pink and white color scheme.

He glanced at his watch. He hadn't planned on this errand taking any more than a few minutes. Actually, he hadn't planned on the errand at all until he'd arrived at the restaurant to find his pastry chef in a tizzy about someone having used his pastry knives to cut meat. He'd tried to calm the high-strung French immigrant, but instead he'd made things worse by referring to him as a cook and the chef had thrown his apron over Ben's head and up and quit.

Friday night and no dessert? A definite no go.

Which had led him straight to the doorstep of the place that had been mentioned along with Benardo's Hideaway in *Hollywood Confidential* that morning.

He considered the fare offered up in the display cases. While all good, they weren't the same crème brûlée and the chocolate cheesecake his customers were used to indulging in.

A dull clang sounded from the kitchen. He imagined that whoever had made the commotion before was cleaning up their handiwork. He looked around for a bell he could ring for service but found none. With a glance at the half dozen other people seated around the place enjoying coffee and reading the paper—he nodded at the one guy in the corner typing madly away on a notebook computer—he stepped toward the stainless steel door to the kitchen and peeked through the window.

A woman's head popped up directly on the other side of the glass, all big hazel eyes, pouty kissable lips and soft blond hair, startling him. Hell, startling them both as she shrieked. He watched as the woman's head disappeared again, followed by more commotion.

Okay...

He stepped back from the door then slid his hands into his pockets. Surely whoever was in there had seen him and would come out to take care of him.

One minute...two minutes...

Ben grimaced. What kind of ship were they running here, anyway?

He tugged his right hand out of his pocket, knocked briefly on the kitchen door, then pushed it slightly open. "Hello?"

Metal clanged to his right. He glanced to where someone stood with their back turned to him at a waist-high stainless-steel counter some twenty feet away.

"Excuse me, could you please tell me if the owner or manager is available?" He stepped farther into the room, noticing how spotless it was, and how large.

The woman turned to face him, her hands filled with tan goo—dough, probably—and he noticed again how attractive she was. Not *Vogue* beautiful. Rather there was something...different about the way her features were put together. From her warm hazel eyes rimmed with some of the thickest lashes he'd seen on a blonde, to her full, quirky lips, she looked like the girl next door and the shop owner's daughter wrapped up into one very delectable package.

"I'm the owner," she said, thrusting one of her hands out. "My name's Reilly..." she trailed off, either unable to remember her last name, or unwilling to share it, "...um, just Reilly." Her plump bottom lip disappeared between white, wonderfully uncapped teeth. "What can I do for you?"

Ben stared down at where she clutched his hand, the warm dough on hers squishing against his skin. He knew the strangest temptation to lift her fingers to his mouth and lick them clean of the sugary concoction, one by one.

"Hello, Just Reilly. I'm Just Ben. And right now I can think of at least a half dozen things I want you to do for me."

2

MOST HOLLYWOOD ACTORS weren't worthy of the film their images were burned onto. In real life they tended to be either shorter than they appeared on the big screen, far thinner, or had skin that without screen makeup was out-and-out cringe material. Of course, Reilly wasn't about to admit to how she came about this knowledge. Namely that she used to be a movie premier groupie as a teen, and that her autograph book boasted no fewer than three hundred autographs, an entire section dedicated to popular movie hunks.

But Ben Kane…

Wow.

No, he wasn't a movie hunk. But that was clearly not because he didn't rate the title. His eyes were… Her breath hitched in her throat. His eyes were, simply, the most gorgeous eyes she'd ever gazed into. They were the lightest of light blue. And she guessed that if someone wronged him, those eyes could turn the person into ice cubes with one glance. But right now they seemed to shimmer with electrical life, sending shivers scooting everywhere along her body and making her feel as if she sat under a sunlamp set on superhigh.

His hair... Her eyes shifted as she unabashedly took him in. His hair was coal-black. No, no, not coal. Raven. Yeah, raven-black. And the short, neat cut he sported made it look as shiny and sleek as a raven's feathers.

And his mouth...

She watched as he lifted his right hand and licked—licked!—the sweet dough she'd gotten on him from the tip of his finger.

Reilly stopped breathing altogether.

"Do you, um, have something I could use to clean up with?" he asked, his voice seeming to rumble from the depths of his wide chest.

"What? Oh!" Reilly looked on the counter that held nothing but sticky bun dough, then lifted her apron, holding out a corner for him. Way the wrong move, she realized all too quickly when his tugging pulled the material tight against the tips of her breasts and set them ablaze.

Speaking of ablaze, her face was probably pinker than the walls in the front room. She nearly ripped her apron from his grip and murmured, "Um, let me get you something more...appropriate."

The minute she turned from him, she seemed able to get her thoughts back under control. And the instant she did, she wanted to crawl under the worktable and continue hiding from the man so many Hollywood actresses and models went gaga over.

Did she need reminding that while she had stars' autographs, Ben Kane had had the stars themselves?

In the biblical sense? Heck, in every sense known to man? Or in this case, woman?

No, she didn't.

She would be fine as long as she didn't look at him.

She gave a mental shrug. So she wouldn't look at him. Yes, that was the ticket.

She dampened a corner of a clean white towel with warm water then handed it to him before putting her own hands under the faucet to clean them.

"So what is it again that I can do for you, Mr. Kane?" she asked, happy that her voice sounded once again like her own.

"Mmm. Yes. You see, my pastry chef left me in the lurch this morning so I need a full array of desserts to serve tonight."

Reilly's brows rose as she purposely took her time drying her hands, her back still to him. "What made you think of me?"

"Oh, I don't know. It might have something to do with the *Confidential.*"

She forgot about not looking at him and looked at him.

Gawd. He looked even better than he had a minute ago, if that was possible. Maybe because this time he was grinning at her. A filthy grin that made her toes curl inside her tennis shoes.

She'd always wondered if swooning was something made up for historical romance novels and period films. But the light-headedness that made her feel like she was swaying on her feet made her think again.

"This is awfully short notice." She did have that charity event this weekend that she had to cook for tonight. If she took this on in addition to that she'd be working nonstop until midnight.

"I understand. And I'm willing to pay whatever price you ask." His blue eyes met her gaze squarely. "So, will you do it?"

No, she thought adamantly.

She looked up into his eyes.

"Yes."

She swallowed hard, wondering why she felt that this wouldn't be the last time she'd be thinking one thing and doing another when it came to the devilishly handsome Mr. Kane.

Whoa.

Ben felt like he'd been knocked back onto his heels. He couldn't put his finger on it, but for some reason the quirky owner of Sugar 'n' Spice made him think of all things sugary and spicy. And when she'd asked what she could do for him, his head had filled with myriad things *he'd* like to do for her, such as make that crooked little mouth of hers open with a gasp or a moan. He cleared his throat. More preferably a moan.

In a town where it seemed everyone had an agenda, Ms. Reilly was a breath of much-needed fresh air. There was not one affected thing about her. He'd bet tonight's take at the restaurant that the highlights in her blond hair were natural. And that she wouldn't be able to lie to save her life. She looked at him with naked interest, not even trying to hide her attraction to him.

"Yes, right then," she said. She patted down the front of her apron, then stuck her short-nailed hand into the left pocket and pulled out a notepad. "What were you looking for?"

He told her, from crème brûlée to double chocolate rum cake, the number he would need and what time he would need the order by.

"I'll, um, also take some of what you have with me now."

She blinked at him.

"You know, from the display case in the other room."

"Oh. Yes, of course." She slid the pad and pen back into her pocket then moved toward the door.

Ben absently rubbed his index finger against his chin as he watched her go. No slow, provocative glide for Reilly. Of course, her tennis shoes might make that a little difficult, but he didn't think she'd ever purposely glided in her life.

Not that it made a difference to his libido. Her lush, curvy little bottom under her beige cords made him think of sticky buns in a whole new light.

She hesitated at the door and looked at him. "Is something the matter?"

Ben lifted his gaze to her face. "Hmm? Oh, no. I

was just thinking…" How nice it would be to drizzle syrup over your backside? "Maybe we should add a cheesecake to the list. If it isn't too much trouble."

"I think I may have one in the freezer."

"Good. Good."

He followed her into the other room where she put together a box bearing her logo then asked him what he wanted.

Dangerous question, that. Especially since at that moment he didn't seem to have a whole lot of control over what came out of his mouth.

Much too soon, she handed him the two boxes she'd filled for him.

"How much?" he asked, putting them down on the counter.

"I'll tally everything up at the end of the night and send an invoice along with the delivery."

"Good." He squinted at her left hand. But of course the bareness wouldn't mean a whole helluva lot. He didn't know a chef or a baker to wear rings while they were working. "What time do you get off?"

Her brows nearly disappeared into her hairline. "Excuse me?"

"Tonight. What time will you be free?"

Her head tilted slightly as if she still didn't understand his question. "And you want to know this information because…"

He grinned at her. "Because I'd like to thank you properly."

And because I'd like to find out if your mouth tastes as sweet as it looks.

"The words are enough."

"You're going to make me spell it out for you, aren't you?"

"I know how to spell 'thank-you.'"

Not the way he had in mind. "I'd like to see you again."

"At midnight?" she said slowly.

"If that's the time you finish up."

"Oh." She stared at him for a long moment, then what he was saying appeared to dawn on her. "Oh! You mean…"

"Yes, I mean."

Her gaze, which had been plastered to his face, moved everywhere but to his face. "I, um, don't think that's such a good idea." She used the corner of her apron that didn't have dough on it to wipe down the counter around the boxes.

"Why not?"

"Why, because—" she furtively looked at him, then back at the counter "—because I finish up late tonight because of the order you gave me and another order I need to have ready by tomorrow morning, and…and…"

"And."

"Well, I don't have time."

"Mmm. Okay, tomorrow night then."

She stared at him as if he'd lost his marbles. "To-morrow's Saturday."

"Yes, it is."

"You don't have plans?"

He chuckled. "Nothing that can't be changed or cancelled."

"So you can go out with me…"

He shrugged. "Or we could stay in…"

"Stay in where?" She quickly lifted her hand. "Don't answer that."

"Tell you what," he said, sliding a business card out of his front pocket. "Do you have a pen?" She looked around the counter then slid one out of her apron pocket. "I'm going to give you my private cell phone number, my home phone number, and, of course, the card has the two numbers to the restaurant on it along with the fax." He handed her the card. "Call me when you've made a decision."

"Even if it's no?"

"Especially if it's no."

She made a face that made her look all the more attractive.

"You know, so I have a chance to change your mind."

She pursed her lips slightly as she stared down at the front of the card, then turned it over to look at the back.

The man who had been typing away on a laptop in the corner neared him. "Excuse me," he mumbled under his breath.

Ben's attention fully on Reilly, he moved to let the guy pass, but apparently picked the wrong direction because the guy plowed into him, spilling coffee all over the front of his shirt.

"Oh, sorry, man," the guy said.

Ben looked at him, wondering why he didn't look very sorry.

"No problem."

Reilly couldn't hide her smile as she handed him a handful of napkins. Ben began wiping at the mess, making sure his assailant had moved out of striking distance before continuing his conversation.

"Actually, if you don't mind, I'd like to bring you dinner tonight," he said to Reilly.

"Tonight?"

"Yes, you know, by way of that proper thank-you I mentioned."

"That's not necessary."

"I think it is." He squinted at her. "Did you say midnight?"

"Yes. I mean, no!" Her cheeks turned the most delicious shade of pink. "I mean, that's really not necessary. Really, it isn't."

He hiked a brow. "Are you passing on a free dinner from one of the most popular restaurants in town?"

"Yes. I mean, no!" She ran her fingers through her bangs, then rested the heel of her hand against her forehead. "What I'm trying to say is that I don't think it would be a very good idea. I'll be exhausted and I probably won't be very good company...."

"I meant I'd have one of my staff drop something off on their way home from work."

"Oh."

"Unless you'd like me to deliver the meal personally?"

"No!" Her shoulders slumped and she tucked her chin into her chest. Moments later he figured she was either laughing or crying. She looked up at him, her laughter filling his ears. "That didn't sound very good, did it?"

"Good thing I have a pretty good ego."

"Big, you mean."

"Mmm." He let the noncommittal sound hang in the air between them.

"Well," he said finally. "I'd better get going."

"Yes, you probably should."

He stared at her.

She gestured toward the boxes. "Some of this needs to be refrigerated pretty quick."

"Of course."

"Of course."

He picked up the boxes. "Call me."

"We'll see."

"Call me," he repeated.

"Okay."

He walked toward the door knowing she probably wouldn't call. But that didn't matter. Whatever reason she had for wanting to avoid him didn't stem from lack of attraction. Because he swore, if he checked, he'd have contact burns from the awareness that had arced between them.

He fully intended to be the one to bring her the food tonight.

And he fully intended for both of them to have dessert....

"DID IT, LIKE, majorly suck to be fat when you were my age?"

Reilly snapped her head up from where she was squeezing sweet dough out of a plastic bag with a star tip into two-inch strips. It was eleven o'clock, she had sent Ben's order to Benardo's Hideaway over six hours ago, and still faced another hour or so of cooking for tomorrow's order.

Add to that her fifteen-year-old niece, Efi, sitting on the clean stainless-steel counter against the wall, swinging her legs and banging the back of her platform shoes against the steel doors asking her bizarre questions, and she saw this as a bad end to a perfectly awful day.

She liked her niece. She really did. She just didn't think she was up to answering her question right then.

"What?"

Efi shrugged, making her short, spiked hair move not at all. "I was just thinking about the picture Mom has of you on the Wall of Fame and was wondering what it felt like to be so fat."

"More like Wall of Shame. I don't know. How

does it feel to have your hair match the walls in the front room?''

Efi made a face, lifting her hand to touch her dyed and gelled-within-an-inch-of-its-life pink hair.

Reilly squeezed three strips in quick succession. "And I wasn't *fat* fat. I was…pleasantly plump.''

"You were fat.''

"I was a hundred and eighty pounds. That's pleasantly plump.''

"Is that why they called you Chubby Chuddy?''

"I see my dear sister has been telling stories about me again.'' She brushed her hair from her eyes with the back of her hand. "Chubby means pleasantly plump.''

"Chubby means fat.''

She eyed her pretty, usually tactful, too-thin niece. It would take a good five years and at least thirty pounds to grow into her tall frame. She had the physical characteristics of the rest of the Chudowski family. Well, aside from the dark Mediterranean eyes and hair she'd inherited from her father.

As for Reilly, she'd been born with the ultimate fat gene. Her mother told her there was one lucky duck in every Chudowski family. No matter how much she'd dieted, or how little she'd eaten, she'd been much heavier than other girls her age.

Until she'd turned eighteen, consulted a dietician and finally dropped the weight.

"It wasn't fun,'' she told her niece. "What time is your sister picking you up again?''

Efi looked at her watch, completely clueless as to what impact her questioning had. "She knocks off at the seafood restaurant at eleven so she should be here any minute now."

"Couldn't be soon enough for me," Reilly murmured under her breath as she finished with the dough then shook the stiffness out of her hands.

Normally Efi was her favorite out of her seven nieces and nephews. You didn't have to twist her arm to work. Say the word and she was there and ready, flinching away from nothing, and seeing to everything with a quick, cheery efficiency that made Reilly smile. You had to stop Efi from working, whereas Tina you needed to light a fire under every five minutes to scare her off the phone or get her to put her nail file away.

"I'm sorry, Aunt Rei," Efi said, pushing from the counter and coming to stand next to her. "Did I hit a sore spot?"

The teen draped her skinny arm over Reilly's shoulders and gave a squeeze. Reilly briefly leaned into her and smiled. "Not only did you hit it dead-on, you delivered a TKO."

"So it sucked being…chubby, huh?"

"Yeah," she said quietly. "It sucked being designated as the class fat girl. The occasional taunts I could handle. The pig noises I could have done without."

"Pig noises? Oh, how rank."

Reilly smiled. "Yeah."

It had been a while since Reilly had thought about that time. Really thought about it. Sure, she'd constantly watched her calories lest she began to regain any of that hard-lost weight. But it had been a good, long while since she'd remembered what it was like to feel uncomfortable in your own skin.

Of course, she also realized that Efi's question wasn't all that had brought back the memories. For some reason her awkward exchange with Ben Kane that morning had made her feel like that fat girl all over again. She'd remembered with horror how the captain of the football team had asked her to the prom in her junior year, and she'd gushingly accepted...only to find out later that day that it had all been a cruel joke. On her.

And Ben Kane represented everything that was that football captain. He was tall and handsome and dated all the best girls in class...in the city. What could he possibly want with her? Her love life wasn't just slow, it was nonexistent. Sure, when she'd first dropped the weight, she'd given her new body a trial run. But the men she'd dated weren't really worth mentioning and made her rethink the casual sex thing since she wasn't really getting anything out of it anyway. Especially once she'd explored her body while in the privacy of her own room and turned herself on more than any of the men she'd dated combined.

But Ben...

God, just looking at him made her want to buy new batteries for her vibrator.

"And that's exactly the reason you should stay away from him," she whispered.

"What was that, Aunt Rei?"

"Hmm? Oh, nothing, Ef. I was just talking to myself."

Out front a horn blared.

"That would be your sister," Reilly said with relief.

"Right on time." She kissed Reilly on the cheek. "You sure you don't want me to stay and help finish this up? I could crash upstairs with you tonight."

Reilly smiled. "Thanks, but I think I can manage. Tell your Mom thanks from me."

"Thanks for what?"

"For talking about my Chubby Chuddy days."

Efi laughed. "I will."

She watched her niece go, pinching off a sloppy end from one of the strips of dough. Then she systematically transferred the lined baking sheets to the industrial-size refrigerator, her mind going over everything that had happened that day, and wandering, as it had almost every five minutes, back to Ben Kane and his tempting offer.

"Get real, Chubby Chuddy. Ben Kane is a calorie-packed double, double chocolate cheesecake and you're on a diet."

But nothing she said could stop her from hungering for him anyway.

3

MIDNIGHT. BEN'S RESTAURANT was closed. The infamous L.A. traffic had slowed to a trickle. The city's residential streets were deserted. And Sugar 'n' Spice still looked inviting, even with the lights dimmed and the tables empty.

Ben reached for the food he'd brought along with him then climbed from his black low-slung BMW convertible roadster. There was no sign of life inside the pastry shop, but having worked in a restaurant for a good deal of his life, he knew that didn't necessarily mean someone wasn't working away in the kitchen. He glanced through the sparkling glass toward the kitchen window. Sure enough, he saw a telltale light shining brightly behind the round pane.

Pure, physical want shot through him at the thought of Reilly being but a short distance away from him. He hadn't been able to get her out of his head all night, no matter how busy and hectic it had gotten at the restaurant. And it had been a good, long while since a woman had had that effect on him. Oh, he might be attracted to a woman, know that at some point he would get together with her, but he had always easily shelved thoughts of her while he attended to work.

But Reilly...

He absently rubbed the back of his neck. His attraction to Reilly seemed to fly in the face of everything he thought he knew about himself. She wasn't six-foot-something with model good looks and a sexual prowess he usually found attractive. In fact, she'd tried to dismantle his interest in her, throw up a roadblock in his pursuit of her, completely unimpressed that he owned one of the hottest eateries in L.A., catering to the hottest celebrities and the who's who of the movie industry.

Of course, he didn't flatter himself that all the women he dated were interested in him and him alone. He was aware of those who gravitated toward him because of the indirect Hollywood connections he had. The people he could introduce them to. The newspapers they could get their pictures in just by attending an event with him. While there were stars that garnered international attention for the roles they played and the salaries they raked in, within Hollywood itself was another form of celebrity status. And Ben prided himself on being a part of it.

No, greater America might not know who he was, but the people that greater America *did* recognize? *They* recognized him. And that power drew some intriguing people his way.

It was worlds away from the gray life he'd led growing up, working in the back of his father's hot-dog stand down on Sunset, where mingling with the customers was not only prohibited, but undesirable. After all, there were only so many things a person could say about a hot dog. And a limited time in which to talk about it as the customers either took the food with them, or wolfed it down right on the spot.

Then his father had had a massive heart attack when Ben was twenty. He'd survived but had decided to retire, and had passed on the three stands he owned to Ben, fully expecting his only child to follow in his footsteps.

Instead, a few years later, Ben had sold the stands and used the cash to open Benardo's Hideaway. And while the menu may have changed over the years, the restaurant's motto didn't. Essentially, everyone who walked through the doors of his place was treated like a star and the real stars who came were anonymous. No photographers, no journalists, no press and no fawning fans allowed.

There was at least one major drawback to his switch in gears, though. His father had never forgiven him for not spending his life handing steamed hot dogs out to rushed customers and had yet to even come to Benardo's Hideaway. The last time Ben had visited him, Jerry Kane had said he wouldn't fit in with the hoity-toity crowd his son catered to and would rather eat a frozen dinner at home—hot dogs being out because of his constant battle against cholesterol.

Ben hadn't even realized the door to Sugar 'n'

Spice's kitchen had opened until he blinked and found Reilly standing staring at him through the other side of the glass.

He grinned, her appearance reaffirming everything he remembered about this morning. Her warm blond hair. Her large hazel eyes. Her curvy, hot body.

Metal scratched as she methodically unlocked the front door then pulled it open.

"Ben," her breath seemed to rush out of her sexy, unpainted mouth on a sigh.

"Reilly." He lifted the bags he held. "Turns out the last of my staff left before I could have them deliver this so I had to make the delivery myself."

The twinkle in her eyes told him she didn't buy the line. And he liked that. In that one instant they connected in a silent, knowing way that didn't need words.

Reilly looked at her watch. "Midnight on the button. You're a man of your word."

"You can call me anything, just don't call me late for dinner."

She smiled at that. "Corny."

"Agreed. Are you hungry?"

She seemed to consider the comment and he wondered if her mind was wandering to other hungers, just as his was as he eyed her appetizing mouth, the soft curve of her neck, her narrow wrists and toned forearms. He found it strange that he was lusting after a woman's forearms. But since Reilly was covered from head to toe in an apron and long-sleeved shirt and pants, there was little else for him to lust after.

She sucked her lower lip in between her teeth, as if the action might help in her decision. For a moment he thought she was going to refuse him, turn him away into the night. Then she said, "Actually, I was just thinking about how I haven't really eaten anything all day. And the thought of having Benardo's delivered...well, it seems suddenly all too appealing."

Ben hiked his brows then grinned, idly wondering where the bumbling chatterbox from this morning was hiding out. She held the door open and he stepped inside, instantly assaulted by the aroma of sweet dough baking and of Reilly's clean-smelling skin as he passed her. He began hefting the bags he held to a table, but she stayed him with a hand that seemed to burn straight through his shirt and scorch his skin. "No. Why don't we go back to the kitchen?"

He caught her looking through the front glass windows at his sports car parked at the curb.

"What? Don't want to be seen with me, Reilly?"

She quickly glanced at him and her cheeks pinkened. "You don't understand. I have these three friends who would never let me hear the end of it if they found out we were here together, alone, in the middle of the night." The left side of her mouth turned up. "And who knows what my family would think."

"And do your friends and family make a habit of driving past your shop in the middle of the night?"

"No. But why take chances?"

He wanted to give her at least a dozen reasons why she should take chances, namely with him, but instead followed her sexy little bottom through the shop and back through the door to the kitchen.

The source for the sweet scent permeating the place became immediately clear as he eyed the sheets of freshly baked—were those unfrosted and unstuffed éclairs?—goodies taking up nearly every inch of free counter space.

"Move one of the trays to the side over there," she said, gesturing toward the middle island. She grabbed a towel, checked inside an oven, then took out yet another tray then switched off the temperature. She looked around for a free space, then propped the oven door open and slid the tray back inside. He handed her the one he'd moved to make room for him and Reilly at the counter and she put that inside the open oven, as well.

She ran her wrist across her forehead and looked at him sheepishly. "I have another cart on order," she told him, gesturing off to the side to where two ten-tray carts were full, "but it hasn't arrived yet."

"You may want to go for two or three more."

"I'm afraid you may be right. I had no idea when I opened this place that business would be so good." She stared at him openly, licked her bottom lip, then gestured toward the island.

Ben made a ceremony out of pulling out a free stool for her, then helping her to climb on top of it, guessing his assistance hindered rather than helped the process but up for any excuse to touch her. She gracefully accepted the offer, then waited as he sat next to her and began pulling items out of the bags. Even as he did so, he wondered what they would be having for dessert. And éclairs, as good as they may be, were definitely not at the top of his list.

REILLY COULDN'T quite bring herself to believe that she was sitting in the middle of her shop kitchen in the dead of night watching yummy Ben Kane serve her up dinner from a restaurant that boasted a three-month waiting list for a table.

No, she had never been to Benardo's Hideaway. Oh, sure, she knew where it was. Situated north of Santa Monica, on a jagged outcropping overlooking the Pacific Ocean, everyone agreed that the view was phenomenal, especially at sunset. And with the ocean-side floor-to-ceiling windows, all diners were guaranteed one hell of a show.

But Reilly understood that even the fantastic view ranked a far second to the number one reason the restaurant was so popular: the famous cuisine Benardo's offered. And as Ben took fine china plates out, she began to see what sort of standards the owner upheld.

No foam cartons for Benardo's. Everything was in rubber-topped glass containers and separate from the foods they would be served with. She swallowed hard as she watched Ben's long, thick-fingered hands lay out a navy blue and gold tapestry placemat, two crystal candle holders complete with candles, linen-wrapped silverware, a gold charger plate, then cobalt blue plates that were edged with a gold Greek key design.

"And here I would have settled for a burger on a paper plate," she murmured.

Ben handed her a crystal glass then poured in a finger of red wine. Which type, she couldn't be sure because the letters on the label of the bottle were covered by the white linen napkin he'd wrapped around it. "Shh," he ordered.

She suppressed a giggle then sipped at the wine. Merlot. A good one at that.

She tried to get a peek inside the dish he was opening, but he held it where she couldn't see.

"Close your eyes."

She widened them instead. "What?"

He grinned at her, making her stomach pitch to her feet. "You heard me."

"And if I don't?"

"Then you don't get any food."

She made a face. Five minutes ago she probably would have pointed him toward the door and sent him on his merry way if he'd told her she'd have to close her eyes. But now that she'd been treated to the full presentation, her curiosity had been ignited and she really wanted to see what he had in store for her.

The key word being see.

She shifted on her stool then closed her eyes. What could he do, really, if she peeked?

She felt cloth settle over her eyelids. She immediately reached for it. "Um, you didn't say anything about a blindfold."

She felt as well as heard him say "trust me" very near her ear. She fought a shiver, but was helpless to prevent it from sliding up her arms then down her back to settle finally between her tightly clenched thighs. He took her silence as acquiescence and continued tying the material around the back of her head, careful not to get her hair caught in the knot.

Oh, boy.

While Reilly knew her kitchen better than she did her upstairs apartment, she felt decidedly strange sitting there, being able to touch everything, smell everything, but not see it. Beyond the scent of the éclairs, the hint of cinnamon that still lingered and the honey syrup she'd used on the sticky buns that morning, she became aware of another pungent food scent and salivated.

"Open your mouth," Ben requested next to her ear.

Reilly's throat closed so tightly she could barely breathe but she somehow managed to part her lips, foggily trying to remember the last time she'd brushed her teeth.

Something rested against her tongue. She was vividly aware of the burst of flavor. Of something cheesy and tangy and spicy. Spots of yellow, orange and red exploded behind her closed eyelids as she closed her lips so Ben could extract the fork.

"Mmm." She'd never connected food to colors before. But without the aid of sight, her mind seemed to compensate in other ways.

"That's my own recipe for brie."

Brie. She'd never had brie before, so had no way to connect it to a different type of cheese. She did, however, decide that she'd been missing out.

"More?" Ben's breath disturbed the hair over her left ear, making her nipples harden and her thighs clench more tightly.

"Definitely…more," she whispered.

There was a heartbeat of a pause, then she heard him moving again, and within moments another bite of the delicious brie was resting against her tongue along with something crunchy and tasting of wheat germ. A cracker? Whatever it was, paired with the brie, it was pure heaven.

"Take a sip of wine." He took her hand and placed the wineglass in her fingers. She slowly drank, then he took the glass back. "Open."

She swallowed hard, her heart beginning to pound at the easy cadence of his words. His voice was deep and more intoxicating than the fine wine. His closeness did strange things to her, making her feel as if she stood in the beam of an electrical current. Her skin felt alive and tingly, her toes were curled up in her tennis shoes, and it seemed to take all of her concentration to keep her breathing from becoming a rasp.

Seafood.

Shrimp.

No, a prawn.

Cooked in a sweet coconut mixture that set her mouth to watering and her throat to humming.

While she'd always been a great lover of food, sweets had always been more her thing. The more sugar the better, was her motto. And her mother had come from a sturdy meat-and-potatoes background, with lots of cabbage stuck in for flavor. Having Ben introduce her to a whole new spectrum of culinary delicacies and tastes made her shiver in anticipation.

She slowly chewed the food. "So, um, how did the desserts go over at the restaurant? I hope there weren't too many complaints?"

"Shh. It's not polite to talk with your mouth full."

She giggled then caught herself. "Who died and made you the manners police?"

He slid the fork inside her mouth again, filling it with a mixture that would take her a half hour to try to identify. Then she felt his breath against her other ear, indicating he was no longer sitting but was moving behind her. "No, I'm just a man hoping you'll let him sample some of your...desserts when I'm done."

Oh, boy...

"In fact, do you mind if I take a little taste now?"

Reilly gasped when she felt his tongue against the

right side of her neck. A long, probing lick that nearly melted her into a puddle at his feet. The sensation was doubly powerful because she hadn't known it was coming.

"Mmm. Just as I thought."

What? she wanted to ask, but found that she couldn't. *Did you pick up baking grit?*

"You taste as good as you look."

She somehow managed to swallow the bite in her mouth and crossed her arms over her breasts in case he could see how very powerfully his attentions were affecting her—that is, making her nipples fully erect. "Sorry to disappoint you."

She heard his chuckle on the left side, throwing her equilibrium off even further. "On the contrary, Reilly, you're the most appetizing thing I've seen…tasted, in a long, long time."

She couldn't help an indelicate snort, the sound ringing loud in the cavernous room.

Oh, now *that* was sexy.

She cleared her throat, wishing she could disappear as easily as the world had behind the blindfold. "Sorry."

"You're determined to ruin this seduction scene, aren't you?" he whispered, making her shiver all over again.

"Is this, um, what this is? And here I thought it was just dinner."

His abrupt chuckle told her he could still be surprised. "It will be if you don't shut up."

He put another forkful of food into her mouth when she might have said something. She ignored his earlier rebuke about talking with her mouth full and said, "You and my mother will have to have a talk. Because she wasn't very good at getting me to be quiet, either."

She felt fingers against her knee and nearly hit her head on the kitchen ceiling.

Had she thought, oh boy? Yes, she had. But this definitely deserved a more panicked one.

Reilly had never been very good with seduction. Neither as the seduced nor the seductress. She'd quickly found out she was too high-strung for that. While she was patient with nearly every other aspect of her life, when it came to sex she liked it fast and hard and spontaneous. Something that didn't require her to think. Or didn't call for her to sit still without squirming for an extended period of time.

"Tell me what you're tasting, Reilly," Ben said.

She realized that she hadn't registered that bite. "I don't know. All I can think about is your hand on my knee."

He moved to her other ear. "Then tell me how you're feeling."

Like I want you to remove your hand. "Like I want to jump out of my skin."

Another quiet chuckle. "Not quite the imagery I was after."

Of course it wouldn't be. He was probably thinking more along the lines of hot ovens and temperature probes. But all she could think about was how... awkward she felt having one of L.A.'s hottest men trying to seduce her.

She whispered, "Sorry. That's all I've got to give."

His fingers budged up the inside of her leg.

Oh, God.

"How do you feel now?"

Like ripping off this blindfold and having my way with you on my kitchen island...

The thought caught Reilly so far off guard that she gripped the sides of the stool to keep from falling off. Was she, inexperienced Reilly Chudowski, really considering taking Ben Kane up on his offer for hot sex?

Yes, she realized, she was.

And as he inched his hand farther up her inner thigh, the desire inched up along with it. Oh, yes. She liked that. She liked that very much. She reached out and grabbed a fistful of his shirt then pulled his mouth down to hers, deciding that his idea of skipping straight to dessert was a pretty good one after all.

4

BEN WOULDN'T BE a man if he hadn't wanted to ratchet things up a notch, but he was wholly unprepared for Reilly's move.

He'd guessed she hid some pretty impressive muscles under all those clothes. As she yanked him against her, his guess proved right on target. And he was helpless to do anything but give her what she wanted as he claimed her mouth, the blindfold still tied tightly over her eyes.

Good God, but she had an incredible mouth. She also knew how to kiss. Not in a practiced way, but in a hungry, uninhibited way that left Ben speechless and motionless, accepting her attentions as she nipped and bit, sucked and licked.

His hand still rested between her thighs. He slid it the little bit needed to meet home plate, taking pleasure in her soft moan as she entwined her fingers in his hair.

As a rule, he didn't like when women messed with his hair. Hey, it took a long time to get it to look like this. But Reilly made the move natural. Made him feel that if she hadn't thrust her hands into his hair, things wouldn't have been right.

She scooted on the stool until her knees were on either side of his hips then gave another yank, nearly knocking him off balance and herself off the stool. When the world stopped spinning briefly, he found himself tightly cradled between her thighs, her corduroy-covered sex pressed insistently against the hardness under his slacks.

It hadn't been all that long ago since he'd been with a woman, although this moment with Reilly made it seem like years. Decades, even. The need that suffused his body and heated his blood made him feel ridiculously like a teen getting his first taste of sex. And, damn it if he couldn't seem to get enough of it. Of Reilly. Of the burning in his groin, the tautness of his muscles, the anticipation of the moment he could bury himself deep inside her.

He realized he hadn't moved his hands from where he'd placed them on her back and immediately remedied the situation, diving for her plump backside and the waist of her pants. He hurriedly undid the knot on her apron then slid his fingers inside the back of her waistband, finally reaching sweet, silken flesh. Meanwhile she fussed and pulled and yanked until his shirt hung out of the front of his slacks and her palms flattened against his abdomen.

Sweet Jesus, but she felt good. Tasted good. Damn good. And he was so hot for her it was impossible to believe that she hadn't been in his life before today. Before now.

He plucked the apron from her and let it drop to

the floor then popped the button on her cords and pulled on the material so the zipper skimmed down by itself. He leaned back slightly to take in the skin he'd revealed, only to see what seemed like a yard of pink cotton topped by a frayed elastic band.

"Wow," he said, not readily recalling having seen underwear that huge since he and his middle school friends had raided a slumber party and gotten into Big Bertha's drawers.

He'd worn the mammoth underwear on his head.

He was thirteen and hadn't known better.

But now…

"Oh…my…God." Reilly seemed to catch on to what he was looking at as she grabbed for her blindfold and peeled it away from one eye to stare at him. "I can't believe…"

She tore the blindfold off then jumped from the stool and began doing up her cords. When she faced him again, she had her apron bunched up in front of her pants and her T-shirt had been pulled down so far he suspected it was permanently damaged.

He grinned at her. "I assume we've finished dessert?"

Reilly ran her hand through her hair several times, her gaze flying everywhere but to his face. "You assume correctly." She briefly squeezed her eyes shut. "I should have listened to my mother."

"Pardon me?"

She shook her head. "Nothing."

Ben knew an acute moment of regret that they

hadn't been able to finish what they'd started. Then again, there was always tomorrow....

A HALF AN HOUR LATER Reilly paced the entire length of her apartment above the shop, alternately smacking the heel of her hand against her forehead and cursing herself in imaginative ways.

"You silly, stupid, unthinking...moron," she muttered, wearing down the matting of her inherited area rugs even further.

What had she been thinking, giving in to her desire to kiss the oh-so-kissable Ben Kane? She knew she wasn't the type of girl that type of guy went in for. She didn't even know what a pore minimizer was, much less own a bottle of the stuff. And her underwear...

She pulled to a halt and stared at the front of her cords. She could almost hear her mother's voice. "And always remember to wear a decent pair of underwear in case you get in an accident."

Reilly made a beeline for her bedroom at the back of the upstairs apartment, undoing her cords as she went so that by the time she reached the room they nearly tripped her where they were bunched down around her ankles.

Knowing Ben had seen this underwear was worse than thirty doctors staring down at her lifeless body and taking in the butt-ugly underpants.

She kicked her cords to the corner of the room then shimmied out of the offensive clothing. She held them up, disgusted. Who, besides her, wore such dreadful underwear? She groaned then stalked to the connecting bathroom and threw them into the old claw-foot tub.

''Oh, but there are plenty of others where those came from,'' she muttered to herself.

She strode back into the bedroom and rifled through her underwear drawer, coming out with a single pair of acceptable bikinis and putting them on before yanking out every last pair of undesirable, repulsive cotton panties. Her eye caught on a brand-new blue-and-white striped pair, then another two pairs of plain white. Okay, so she could still use them as period panties. But the rest of them? They had to go.

Hands full, she stalked back to the bathroom and dumped the offending underwear into the bathtub with the other pair, not stopping until she stood above the pile with lighter fluid and matches. Only she was unprepared for the huge flame that shot out from the mess, licking at her fabric shower curtain, determined to take that with them, as well.

Oh boy…

The smoke alarm in the hall began buzzing as she reached to turn on the faucet then used the handheld showerhead to attack the threatening flames.

Great, just great. Only she could nearly burn the house down trying to destroy any evidence of the ugliest underwear known to man. So what if they were comfortable? So what if they were affordable? Ben Kane had *seen* her in them.

She put the last of the flames out, gave the smoldering black pile another squirt of water, then went out into the hall to fan at the earsplitting alarm. Over the racket, she made out pounding on her door. She looked in that direction. The building stood apart from the others and hers was the only one that boasted an apartment overhead. She groaned. If it was Ben, she'd die. Just absolutely die.

Coughing, she rushed to open the door that overlooked the back alley and that was accessible by an iron-wrought staircase, to find herself staring at one of her regular customers.

"Johnnie!" she said. Computer geek Johnnie Thunder was the last one she expected to see on her doorstep at this time of night.

"Is everything all right?" he asked, trying to look beyond her.

Reilly fanned at the smoke filling the apartment. "Fine. Everything's fine. Just a little…accident in the kitchen, that's all."

Oh, that was grand. Her, a baker, setting fires in the kitchen. If her insurance company ever found out she'd said that, her premiums would go through the roof.

"What are you doing here, anyway?" she asked.

Johnnie's gaze lowered. Seemed she had forgotten to put her pants on over her skimpy bikinis.

Oh, why couldn't it have been Ben at the door?

She reached for a magazine and held it over herself.

Johnnie said, "I heard the smoke alarm across the street. You know, from my apartment."

She hadn't known he lived across the street. "Oh." She smiled. "Sorry to have disturbed you. I'm sure the stupid thing will stop just as soon as I get some of this smoke out of here."

"Do you need some help?"

"No!" Rcilly bit her bottom lip then sighed. "I mean, thank you, but it's nothing I can't handle, really."

"Are you sure?"

Oh, yes. The last thing she wanted was for him to discover what she'd really been doing. "Positive. See you in the morning."

He nodded. "In the morning, then."

Reilly closed the door after his retreating back then collapsed against the hardwood. The smoke alarm finally shut off, leaving the apartment almost eerily silent and smelling like acrid smoke. It would probably take a month for her to get rid of the smell.

Which was no less than she deserved, she supposed. I mean, who forgot they were wearing granny panties when there was a remote chance that one of the hottest guys in L.A. might be stopping by at midnight?

Her, that's who. And she wasn't very happy with herself about it.

"Fate," she whispered.

Yes, that's what it was. She hadn't been fated to sleep with someone of Ben Kane's impressive caliber so fate had stepped in to interrupt. To remind her of who she was, who she used to be, and who she would never be with.

She clamped her eyes shut. Just once. Just once she would liked to have gone out with the captain of the football team.

And just once she would have liked to have had sex with Ben Kane.

"Not in this lifetime." Reilly tossed the magazine back onto the hall table then stepped back toward the bathroom and the mess there. Better a little mess now then a big mess later, a quiet voice in her head said.

"Tell that to my raging hormones," she responded.

Even as she scooped the charred cotton out of the tub and into the wastebasket, she wondered where that gift was that Mallory had given her a year or so ago. The one that took fifty dollars worth of batteries and could give a jackhammer a run for its money. She figured that nothing less would be able to take Ben's place in her bed that night. Though she suspected even the deluxe vibrator wouldn't come close.

Something clattered in the alley outside. She slowly straightened, straining to hear. Was Johnnie still out there in case she should change her mind and need his help?

Another clatter, this time closer. Reilly jumped. She slowly put the wastebasket down, searched around the bathroom, then picked up a can of aerosol hairspray. She made her way back out to the door and wrapped her fingers around the knob. If it was Johnnie, she'd just tell him…what? That she'd been fixing her hair?

Oh, this is ridiculous, she thought. It was probably just a mouse or something.

Still, she gripped the can tightly as she swung the door inward.

Nothing. Not even a breeze disturbed the night.

She made a face and dared stick her head outside, looking from the left to the right. Not a person to be seen.

She dropped the can to her side and sighed. She was losing it. Really, she was.

The door was nearly closed when she heard a loud screech. She jumped and began spraying. Only the black scrap of fur that she had nearly closed the door on was already inside her apartment, watching her.

A cat.

She rested a hand over her loudly beating heart. ''You scared the bejesus out of me,'' she whispered, taking in the battered feline. Getting caught in a door looked like it was far from the worst that had happened to the bedraggled black cat. Tufts of fur were missing from his back and hindquarters. Cats didn't molt, did they?

Reilly opened the door again. ''Go on, now. Scat.''

The cat didn't move. Worse, it sat down, twitching its tail at her.

''Come on, now. It's too late for this.'' Nothing. ''If you go back outside I'll give you some milk.''

The cat got up and meowed, but made no move toward the door.

Reilly looked back outside, then closed the door again. "Fine. You want to bunk here for the night, I'm okay with that. But first thing in the morning, you go." She put the hairspray down then headed for the kitchen where she put out milk and a half can of tuna. "And no complaints about the smell. It's a long story."

The cat shied away from her touch, but the instant she began scratching its ears, it leaned into her palm. Reilly smiled.

"Welcome to my house, Cat," she said softly.

THE FOLLOWING DAY Ben looked over one of his shipping invoices again. Sure enough, he'd been delivered two hundred pounds of octopus instead of crab legs when Alaskan crab legs were the special tonight.

He rubbed his thumb and forefinger over his closed eyelids and counted backward from ten to keep from losing it with the clueless deliveryman. This was the fourth such screwup so far this morning, and the day was young yet. From a cheap coffee liqueur instead of Tia Maria to rump roast instead of steaks, his stockroom was growing full of stuff he didn't need and didn't want.

"What do you want me to do, boss?" asked Lance Dickson, the floor manager who had taken the first three wrong orders.

He looked at the deliveryman. "Take it back."

"And the crab legs?" Lance asked.

"I don't know," he said absently. "Maybe we'll tell them there was another oil spill in Alaska or something and hopefully we'll have some in next week." They both knew how quasi-environmentalist the L.A. community was. "Right now I want you to get on the computer and double check whatever else is due to come in today."

Lance saluted him. "Right on it, boss."

Ben shook his head. Definitely not the type of thing you wanted to face when you hadn't had much sleep the night before. After Reilly had all but chased him out of her shop then slammed the door on his grinning face, he hadn't been able to get her or her underpants out of his mind.

He stepped down the hall to the back of the restaurant, blinking his eyes at the relative dimness in the large, rough-hewn wood-lined dining area. He just didn't get it. Under normal circumstances, catching a glimpse of such unattractive undergarments would have had a detrimental effect on his libido. But his reaction to Reilly was turning out to be anything but normal. In fact, when he finally had fallen asleep, he'd had dreams of getting those underpants wet and watching the cotton cling to her swollen womanhood and firm behind. And he'd asked her to keep them on as he positioned her on top of him and watched her bear down on his pulsing erection.

He'd awakened to suspiciously damp sheets to find

he hadn't set his alarm clock. After stripping his sheets, his day had only gotten worse.

He now crossed to the door where a black chalkboard hanging inside advertised fresh Alaskan crab legs, and he rubbed off the selection.

Despite the dark cloud over the day so far, strangely enough all he had to do was think of Reilly and he'd find himself grinning like an idiot.

He rounded the empty bar then picked up the telephone and put it on the counter before looking for the card to Sugar 'n' Spice he'd slipped into his pocket that morning.

"Sugar 'n' Spice and everything nice," a young woman's voice answered.

Ben frowned, sure it wasn't Reilly. He couldn't imagine her saying those words. "Is Reilly there, please?"

A pause, then, "May I ask who's calling?"

"A restaurant owner who would like to place an order," he answered, grinning.

"Oh. Just a minute."

Was it him, or did she sound disappointed?

"Sugar 'n' Spice."

Ah, Reilly. "Good morning. How are you and your underpants doing this morning, Ms. Reilly?"

"Oh, God." He heard the squeak of door hinges and guessed she'd ducked into the kitchen of the shop. "I can't believe you're calling me here."

"Where would you have me call you?"

"Nowhere. Ever again. Just let me die in peace without remembering what happened last night."

Ben carried the phone to the end of the bar. "Don't you mean what didn't happen?"

"That, too." He heard her swallow hard. "Look, is there something specific you wanted?"

"Why?"

"Why? Well, because…because, I have a long line of people waiting for service and my niece Tina is giving me the evil eye."

"The evil eye?"

"It's a Greek thing. Oh, never mind."

"Actually, there is a reason I'm calling."

A pause. "And?"

"And what?"

"And the reason is?"

"I'd like to repeat yesterday."

"Repeat yesterday as in…"

"As in…everything."

"Not a chance in hell."

"I thought you'd already agreed to supply desserts for the restaurant until I could find a replacement pastry chef."

"Oh, that. Of course. My word is my bond."

Ben's grin widened. His own personal motto.

"And you'll be finishing up at midnight?"

"No."

The grin left his face. "What time will you be finishing, then?"

"Around six."

"Good then, I'll—"

"You'll nothing. I'm going out."

Ben knew a heartbeat of hesitation along with an unhealthy helping of jealousy. "Do I know him?"

"Her."

Ben's brows rose.

"Well, that sounded good, didn't it?" She laughed. "Her as in my fifteen-year-old niece, Efi. We have a longstanding date for a night in front of the television tonight. Just us, some popcorn and a stack of DVDs."

"I could cater for you."

"No!"

"Didn't like the food?"

He heard a gusty sigh. "The food was great, Ben. Thanks for bringing it. It's just…"

He sat down on a stool on the other side of the bar, reminding him of how she'd looked sitting on a similar stool in her kitchen, blindfolded and oh so hot for him. "It's just…what?"

Another sigh. "It's just that I don't think it would be a good idea for us to see each other…personally again."

"Again? As in never again?"

"Uh-huh."

"Not acceptable."

She didn't say anything and for a moment he was afraid she'd hung up.

"Tomorrow night, then," he suggested.

"No."

"The night after that."

"No."

"Thursday, Friday, Saturday."

"No, no, no." Silence. "What happened to Wednesday?"

"That's the night I'm having you to the restaurant for a special dinner made for two."

"No."

"Good. I'll pick you up at around seven. I'm guessing you live above your shop, right?"

"No."

"Very good, then. Dressy casual. Oh, and wear a pair of those sexy underpants again, will you? They do something to me."

He heard her hang up and chuckled, slowly hanging up the phone on his end, feeling better than he had in a long, long time.

"Boss?"

He looked up to find Lance standing in the doorway.

"Every order we have in is screwed up. What do you want me to do?"

Ben reached over and put the phone on the other side of the bar. "Fix them, of course. You take half, I'll take the other. And at some point maybe we'll figure out what in the hell happened."

5

"WHAT WAS ALL THAT ABOUT?" Tina asked when Reilly came out of the kitchen and hung up the phone.

Reilly fixed her hair then straightened her apron. "What was all what about?"

Her eighteen-year-old niece slid the tray of cream horns back into the display case, her dark eyes narrowed. "I've never seen you take the phone in the kitchen."

"Uh-oh," another voice sounded from the table near the window. The same table that held her three friends, gathered for morning coffee, sticky buns and conversation. Layla was there, as were Mallory and Jack.

"What? What am I missing?" Layla asked, looking at Mallory then Jack then lastly at Reilly.

"Not a thing. You're not missing a thing," Reilly said before Mallory could speak, then retook her stool at the table while Tina sighed with exaggerated agitation.

The shop was mostly empty at this time of morning, a brief lull between the early birds and the late risers. Johnnie Thunder was connected to his laptop in the corner. Being Saturday, Tina didn't have classes, so she'd volunteered to help out now, then take the van to drop off the éclairs at the caterers at eleven.

"Just as I thought. It was him, wasn't it?" Mallory asked, openly licking her fingers of sticky bun syrup.

Next to her family, Reilly's friends meant more to her than any three people in the whole world. Layla Hollister was a doctor at a free clinic not too far from the shop. She was engaged to marry another doctor— a chop doc, though Reilly did have to admit that Sam Lovejoy wasn't your run-of-the-mill plastic surgeon—in a little over a month. With dark hair and green eyes, she was everything that every woman longed to be. Tall, slender, beautiful and nice.

Then there was Mallory Woodruff, documentary producer, who was what every woman was afraid she might turn into. With her wavy, untamed dark hair, pale skin and huge eyes, Mall was a petite stick of dynamite just looking for a place to go off. She had a penchant for wearing T-shirts designed to get a re-action—today's read God Made Men to Amuse Women—and had a chip on her shoulder the size of Mount Everest.

Then there was Jack.

Reilly looked at him and instantly smiled. A columnist for *L.A. Monthly*, Jack was drop-dead gorgeous with light brown hair and crinkly moss-green eyes. When the four of them had met three years ago, at a disaster drill they'd all thought was real, Reilly, Layla and Mallory had sworn an oath that to preserve their budding friendship, none of them would go after Jack. Reilly was awfully glad they had because she couldn't imagine their circle without Jack, and his snug jeans and denim shirts, in it.

Layla snapped Reilly back to the here and now and the uncomfortable conversation Mallory had lured her into.

"Him who? Would somebody please tell me what's going on?" Layla asked.

Jack mumbled something under his breath. "Don't we all have enough to worry about without adding to the mix? I'm getting a refill."

All three women watched him go. Simply because it was so much fun to do so. Especially since he knew they were watching him. They could make out his curses as he walked.

"Ben Kane," Mallory said.

Layla nearly toppled her stool over she sat back so quickly. "What? Not *the* Ben Kane? The infamous Ben Kane of Benardo's Hideaway fame? The same Ben Kane who was mentioned in the *Confidential* piece along with our dear friend yesterday morning?"

"Say his name like he's a nationally recognized trademark again and I'm going to smush a sticky bun into your neat white blouse," Mallory threatened.

Layla's answering smile made Reilly smile back.

"Anyway, I thought we were here to discuss weddings—namely Layla and Sam's—and bridesmaid dresses—namely mine and Mallory's?"

Layla sipped her coffee. "There's always time for

talk about Ben Kane.'' She looked to Mallory. ''What happened?''

Mallory shrugged. ''He came in yesterday.''

Layla looked disappointed. ''Is that all?''

Both women looked at Reilly expectantly. ''What do you want me to say? That his pastry chef quit? That he cleaned out my display case then ordered a whole bunch of other stuff? That I was wearing my granny underpants and the instant he saw them he ran full-out in the opposite direction?''

Jack had returned to the table, stopped cold, then turned around again and started toward Johnnie Thunder, apparently craving some man speak.

Mallory held up a hand. ''Whoa, whoa, whoa. How did we get from cleaning out your display case to his seeing your enormous undies?''

Reilly hated that her friend knew what kind of underwear she wore. ''Never mind. It's not going to happen again, so there's no sense in even going there.''

''Oh, please go there. If just so Mall and I can enjoy the trip,'' Layla said.

To her surprise, Reilly found herself sharing every last detail from the night before. From how Ben had shown up at her shop at midnight, fed her dinner—she conveniently left out the blindfold part because she still wasn't sure how she felt about that herself—to how he'd gotten an eyeful of her underwear then beat a hasty retreat.

''Oh, God,'' Layla said, horrified. ''I probably

would have killed myself if that had happened to me."

Mallory grimaced. "No, you wouldn't. Granny panties are not suicide material. After all, look what they landed Bridget Jones."

Reilly and Layla stared at her. "It got her heart broken by a womanizing loser," Layla said.

"Yes, but it was Hugh Grant. As far as losers go…" She seemed to realize what she was saying and made a face. "Anyway, that's neither here nor there. The fact remains is that he wanted to see your underwear, period. And that you let him."

Reilly stared down into her black coffee.

"And that he just called," Mallory finished.

Layla's head snapped to. "Yes! What did he want?"

Reilly shrugged. "To confirm today's order."

"Liar," Mallory accused.

Reilly was secretly delighted that Ben had asked her out. Well, not too secretly because she caught her friends sharing a grin.

"Is it safe to come back now?" Jack asked, hesitating near his stool. "I've had enough cyber lingo to last me at least the rest of the day."

Layla laughed. "Do so at your own peril."

He sat down again. "I know Ben Kane."

All three women stared at him.

"What? I did a piece on him about a year ago. If you guys read my column, you'd know that."

Mallory raised her right hand. "I read every last one of your columns, God as my witness."

Jack grinned at her. "At least I have one faithful friend."

"That doesn't really qualify as knowing him," Layla pointed out. "Your doing a column on him."

"Well, then, how about I share that I was one of his first customers and that he has a lunch sandwich named after me at the Hideaway?"

"He does not," Reilly said.

"Does, too." He shrugged. "Of course, it helps to have a name like Jack Daniels."

"So when are you two going out again?" Mallory asked Reilly.

Jack said, "Well, we've never actually dated. Only hung out."

Mallory rolled her eyes.

"I told you," Reilly said. "Never."

She just needed to stop thinking about the invite to his restaurant. The invite that she didn't respond to one way or the other. The invite that she'd be crazy to accept. The invite that she wanted to snap up if only to see Ben again and show him her new, sexy underpants.

"Hmm," Mallory said, watching her a little too closely.

"Oh, God, is that the time?" Layla asked, looking at her watch then scooting from the stool. "I promised I'd be at the clinic ten minutes ago.'' She slung her purse over her shoulder. ''So we're agreed on the dresses?''

Mallory and Reilly made a face. They both hated the dresses, but then again what percentage of brides- maids usually liked their dresses?

''So we'll meet for a first fitting on Wednesday at eleven then,'' Layla said, then shot for the door with- out waiting for an answer.

''Get the woman laid and she turns into Attila the Hun,'' Mallory said, nearly causing Jack to spew his coffee out over the newspaper he was reading.

She grabbed him by the sleeve. ''Get a disposable cup. You've got to drive me to scout out some shoot- ing sites.''

''What happened to your car?'' Reilly asked.

''Finally bit the dust once and for all,'' Jack an- swered for Mallory.

''You can borrow my van, Mallory,'' Reilly of- fered. ''Well, after Tina makes some deliveries.''

Her dark-haired friend smiled at her. ''Thanks, but no. I think I enjoy terrorizing Jack more. You know, since he doesn't have a real job and all.''

Jack's back stiffened as Mallory led him toward the door. ''Being a magazine columnist is a real job. In fact, you can't get any more real. Just the other day…''

Reilly watched the door close after her friends, shook her head, then started cleaning up the table.

"OH, HE'S SO CUTE!" Efi cried when Reilly let her into the apartment upstairs later that night. "When did you get a cat?"

"I didn't. And he's not cute. He's the butt-ugliest thing I've ever laid eyes on." Reilly watched her fifteen-year-old niece pick up the scraggly feline from where he'd been sprawled out in the middle of the coffee table. She idly wondered where else she was going to find black hair.

Efi looked at Reilly as she fussed over the old Tom, then told her, "You know, I've decided that I'm going to grow up to be just like you."

Reilly put down her purse and the leftovers they'd brought home from a local Italian restaurant they'd just eaten dinner at. "How do you mean? Independent? Free-spirited? Successful?"

"Single with a cat."

Reilly's hands froze where she was going through the mail. Yikes! Details aside, that's exactly what she was, wasn't it? She'd turned into every woman's nightmare.

She eyed the cat, deciding it had to go. The single thing she might not be able to do much about. But the cat, she could.

"If you like him so much, take him home with you."

Efi made a face. "I would but Mom's allergic."

"Your mom had a cat growing up," Reilly told her.

"I know. Mittens. But now she's allergic."

"I bet." Reilly put the mail down, retrieved a couple of diet caffeine-free sodas from the fridge, then sat down on the sofa. "So tell me what's made you decide to become an old spinster like your aunt?"

The cat leaped out of Efi's skinny arms and her niece plopped down on the couch next to her, sighing dramatically as she took a soda. "Mom thinks it's because, you know, it's nearing that time of the month."

Reilly still couldn't seem to accept that her young niece was menstruating already. "And the truth is?"

"Jason Turner."

"Ah. A boy."

Efi paused as she took a sip of her soda. "Not a boy. A full-grown man." She frowned. "Well, almost anyway. He's eighteen."

Reilly paused then affectionately punched her niece's shoulder. "And too old for you."

Efi shrugged. "He's a senior at school and has the biggest blue eyes you've ever seen and when he smiles I swear I go weak in the knees...and...and..."

"And he doesn't know you exist."

Efi deflated against the cushions. "Actually he did notice me today. He stopped in the hall to say that I'd chosen an interesting color for my hair. That I matched the curtains in the gymnasium."

Reilly cringed. "Ouch."

Efi nodded. "I hate Greek school."

"Why Greek school? I got the impression that this happened at public school."

"It did, but if I didn't have to go to Greek school

I could hang out at my real high school more and maybe see Jason more often.'' She sulked. ''I hate Greek school.''

Reilly hugged her to her side. ''You don't hate Greek school.''

''You sound just like mom. And I do, too, hate Greek school.''

''Tell me why?''

''You got an hour?''

''Actually, I do. You see it's Saturday night and my niece is staying over and I happen to have nothing but time on my hands.'' She put her feet up on the coffee table. ''Just remember we have that DVD to fit in.''

''Let's watch the DVD.''

''Let's talk about life as Efi first.''

Her niece sighed in a way only an angst-filled fifteen-year-old could. God, Reilly would never relive that time in her life if you paid her a million dollars.

Efi laid her head back against the sofa. ''Which part do you want to hear? About how I can't play softball with the rest of the girls in my class because I have to go to Greek school on Wednesdays to learn how to say 'I want a loaf of bread' in Greek? This when my mom can't speak a word of Greek to save her life? No, wait, let's talk about how I can't go to my best friend's house because her father's a minister and Dad's afraid it will confuse me? Then there's how I'm in a class at Greek school with kids of all ages and the only others even close to me in age are Shy

Sotiria and Fat Fodos, and both of them think I'm weird.''

Reilly picked at the spikes on Efi's head. "Sorry, honey, but I think everyone probably thinks you're a bit on the strange side right now."

She remembered the day last week when Efi had dyed her hair with some sort of home kit she'd bought from the drugstore. Her sister had called to blame her for the overt act of rebellion. "You encourage her! Talking to her like she's an adult. She's just a kid, Rei. She needs guidance."

Reilly believed that she got enough guidance from her parents. What this girl needed was a little unconditional TLC. And she provided it whenever she could.

"Then, of course, there's Jason," Reilly prompted.

Efi groaned. "You would have to bring him up."

"And what about the boys at Greek School?"

Efi crossed her arms over her modest chest. "There are no boys at Greek school. None worth mentioning. Anyway, they all think I'm weird, too. Besides, I don't put out so I'm not even popular in that way, either."

Reilly nearly choked on her soda.

Efi patted her on the back. "Are you all right?"

She nodded and took several deep breaths. Is that why she hadn't been popular in school, either? Because she hadn't "put out," as her niece had so not nicely put it.

No, it had been because she'd been fifty pounds overweight.

And, she realized, she still dressed like she was that fat girl…at least up until last night and Ben Kane.

She felt like groaning right alongside her heartsick niece.

She remembered Layla saying once how she believed childhood was something to be survived. Thinking about it now, she wondered how much of the child still resided in herself. Was she, deep down in her heart of hearts, still that fat girl hoping to stay under the radar, who panicked when anyone noticed her?

She and Efi looked at each other.

"DVD," they said in unison.

And that's where the conversation about Jason and thoughts of Ben ended.

Well, for the next five minutes anyway.

6

TWO DAYS LATER, Reilly ducked out of sight where she sat in the driver's seat of the shop minivan, peeking through the window where Ben stood in the backdoor of Benardo's Hideaway accepting a shipment from a beer supplier. It was 6:00 a.m. on a Monday morning, and her only hired help, Tina, had called in sick. In fact, Efi had told Reilly that Tina and a few friends had gone on a spur-of-the-moment road trip to San Francisco, ditching classes and work. So there Reilly sat hiding from the one man she didn't want to see her so early on a Monday morning.

Who would have thought Ben Kane would be up so damn early, anyway? Surely he had people who saw to this kind of business for him? Who made it possible for him to sleep in? To live the life of privilege every magazine and newspaper suggested he lived?

And her? Well, one of Tina's stunts was enough. She was going to advertise for a part-time deliveryman the instant she got back to the shop. All of this running around when she should be back at the shop getting ready to open the doors was hell on the nerves.

A brief rap on the window. "Reilly?"

She snapped upright so quick she hit her elbow on the steering wheel. Standing next to her door was none other than Ben Kane himself, looking twice as delectable as anything her shop had to offer. Which was bad enough. What made it doubly worse was that she knew she looked like death warmed over. Three nights without much sleep, and lying next to a cat that purred louder than a Mack truck, could do that to a person.

A man like Ben Kane could do that to a person.

She rolled down her window and pushed her disheveled hair from her face. "Uh, hi!" she said with forced cheer. "Imagine seeing you here."

His half grin hit her with full impact. "I, um, own the joint. Where would you have me be?"

Oh, I don't know, Reilly thought. Home in bed with whatever model you picked up last night, maybe?

"Right," she said instead, nodding stupidly, feeling even dumber yet that she'd been hiding in the front seat of a van that was clearly marked Sugar 'n' Spice.

She pushed open the door of the ten-year-old minivan painted white with pink lettering and nearly caught Ben clean in the stomach. "Oh, God! Sorry," she said. "Are you all right?"

"Believe it or not, this isn't my first experience with a rogue delivery truck door. Only usually the other guys mean it."

Reilly returned his smile, feeling all sugary inside now that she was standing next to him.

She had forgotten how tall he was. How utterly yummy. Especially when he was looking at her like he had forgotten all about the granny underpants and could only think about what lay underneath.

She scrambled to recall which panties she'd put on this morning. The ice-blue ones. The thin, satiny ice-blue ones that kept disappearing up her butt cheeks and that she kept having to dig out.

She caught her hand moving to do just that and stopped herself. First granny panties, now grabbing for her butt. Boy, was she ever making a good impression.

"I, um, have today's orders," she mumbled under her breath.

"Where's Tina?"

Ben easily closed the door and followed her quick steps with a long, leisurely, all-too-handsome stride. "AWOL. And since someone has to be there to man the shop, now is the only time I had available to bring this over before the lunch crowd hits you and…" Reilly realized she was babbling and snapped her mouth shut. She didn't babble. She never babbled.

And what was that odd sound? Her arm hairs were standing on end at the hum of a skilled saxophone player. Making her want to run in the other direction, away from the sound, away from the reaction.

Or was she just imagining it?

"Are you playing music in the bar?"

Ben blinked his light, light blue eyes at her. "No. And it's a restaurant. Not a bar."

They both looked around. The last truck had already pulled out leaving them standing alone in the lot with nothing but the sound of the ocean over the side of the hill.

So what was that sound then?

Ben shrugged and said, "I could have sent someone over to your place to pick up the delivery."

But then I wouldn't have had a chance to sneak around, Reilly thought.

"I didn't want to be a bother," she said instead. She waved her hands as she continued to try to outrun the sound of the sax. She ducked behind the van. "Anyway, I have a couple of other deliveries to make, as well, so this was on the way."

Benardo's Hideaway was not on anyone's way. It was a destination, not a journey.

"I just didn't expect to see you, that's all," she said, then widened her eyes at the blurted words. She hadn't meant to say that. So why had she?

She moved to open the back van door. Ben rested his hand against it and held it shut. "Yes, but you were hoping you would, weren't you?"

Were all men made as sexually confident as Ben Kane, or were they trained somewhere to be that way?

Reilly swallowed hard when he hooked the index finger of his other hand in the front of her jeans. "Have you taken a good look at me this morning? Do I look like a woman on the make?"

He slowly shook his head. "Which makes you all the more provocative."

Provocative. No one had ever used the word to describe her before. And while she would never have described herself in those terms, Ben's saying the words made her feel that way. Made her pout her lips in a way she hadn't realized she knew how to do, thrust her breasts out just a tad more and widen the stance of her feet.

Provocative…

Boy, did she ever want to provoke a reaction in Ben Kane in that one moment.

He tugged on the waist of her jeans as if trying to get a look inside.

Provocative evaporated leaving humiliation behind. Reilly swatted at his hand. "What are you doing?"

His grin widened. "Trying to get a peek at what you have on under there today."

"Normal underwear," she managed to squeeze out of her tight throat. The truth was, the back of his finger was resting against her bare stomach, causing all kinds of unfamiliar chaos to swirl around in there. "Normal underwear that you're not going to see."

He curved his finger tighter into her jeans. "Oh, come on. Throw a man a bone, Reilly. I haven't been able to get your underpants out of my mind since I saw them."

Her face burned hotter…along with other parts of her she was determined to ignore. "Bones are for dogs. So stop acting like one." She cleared her throat.

"And I hope you have a good memory, because it's going to have to last you."

Was it her, or had he moved closer to her?

"Until when?"

Oh, boy. He *had* moved closer. And he was eyeing her pouting mouth like he was a millisecond away from kissing it.

Reilly licked her lips. "Until the next Ice Age, at least."

"Mmm. At least we'll know that with the kind of underpants you wear, you'll be warm enough."

Reilly's bark of laughter surprised even her.

She hadn't wanted to laugh. When she laughed, she dropped her protective barriers. And did she ever need all the help she could get when dealing with the irresistible likes of Ben Kane.

He rested his forehead against hers, mesmerizing her with his eyes. "Tell me, Reilly, why are you so determined to deny the attraction between us?"

"I don't know…because you're double chocolate cheesecake and I have a cavity?" Oh, how she wished he would kiss her already. "Actually, when it comes to you I have a whole mouthful of cavities."

His gaze dropped to her lips. "Sounds painful."

"You have no idea…"

She felt the finger inside the waist of her jeans dip lower…and lower still, stealing her breath away.

"So why not go to the dentist and have them taken care of?"

She shook her head as much as she could while

they were still connected at the temple. "Be-cause...because...because dentists scare the crap out of me."

You scare the crap out of me.

And I'm tired of waiting for you to kiss me so I'm going to kiss you.

Then Reilly was draping her arms around his neck, lifting up on the tips of her toes, and plastering her mouth against his.

A groan wound around the inside of her body, a sigh that served as a buffer between them and the rest of the world. For that one moment, what she was doing felt so damned right it was hard to believe it could be wrong. But it was that wrongness that made her heart ache even as the rest of her cried out for more of the man pressing against her.

The sound of that smoky sax seemed to grow louder as she licked his top lip, then his bottom, then set out to devour his entire mouth.

Mouths didn't come more decadent than Ben Kane's, she decided. She could stand there kissing him for hours. Days, even. A languid desire swam through her veins as she turned her head this way and that, licked and kissed and nipped. Then the finger at her waist dove even lower until it finally hit pay dirt in the form of her tiny panties. She shivered, wanting him to move lower still. Yes, yes, that's it. Just a little to the right and...

His finger burrowed into the top edge of her panties, brushed against her tight bud, then slid into the wetness beyond.

Oh, yes…

"Boss, there's a guy on the phone who says someone's… Oh, sorry."

While Ben hadn't made a move to break the connection, Reilly leaped away from him like she'd just suffered an electrical shock. The sax abruptly stopped playing. His finger disappeared from her jeans. But unfortunately the heat he'd ignited continued to burn, even more brightly than before. She glanced at the guy in the doorway of the restaurant, then back at Ben, only vaguely noting that the guy had disappeared back inside.

Ben's gaze hadn't budged. "Get back here," he murmured.

She shook her head. "I take it your staff is used to you mauling women in the parking lot."

He chuckled quietly, making her shiver all over. "If I recall correctly, you were the one mauling me." He glanced down to the front of his slacks. "As for my staff…he would be very happy if you continued."

Reilly was glad he was facing away from the restaurant because the front of his slacks was tented out so high she had to swallow a gasp.

He said, "No? I was afraid you'd say that." He dropped his hand to the van's back door handle and pulled it up and open. "You wouldn't happen to have anything frozen in there, would you?"

Reilly reached inside and took out a tub of French

vanilla ice cream she'd brought along to go with the caramel drizzled apple pie. "Here. Try this. Oh, wait." She found an apron off to the side and wrapped it around the sweating carton. "We, um, wouldn't want to cause a wet spot or anything."

Ben threw back his head and laughed so heartily she couldn't help but laugh with him. "True," he said. "Not with ice cream, anyway."

The very air between them seemed to shimmer with longing as Reilly gazed at him. She couldn't remember a time when she'd felt so…connected to another human being. So on the same page. Of course it would help if she could get rid of the survival instinct to grab an eraser.

"Come in for coffee," Ben murmured.

"I…can't." She broke the connection. "Besides, you forget that I have to get back to the shop to serve coffee to others."

"Maybe you should consider changing your hours."

She raised her brows. He wasn't…surely he couldn't be…was he suggesting something that would stretch their connection beyond this one moment of attraction?

"Hmm," she said, pushing the ridiculous thought aside. He was teasing her. He always seemed to be teasing her. "I don't think my customers will go for being served morning coffee at three in the afternoon."

"Noon, then."

Reilly took a step backward before the desire to kiss him could hit her full force again. "Are you trying to run me out of business, Ben Kane?"

"Nope. I'm just trying to chase you closer to me."

She searched his eyes. A cheesy line, no doubt. But did he mean it? He couldn't possibly mean it.

She figured the safest possible reaction would be to ignore her first reaction. "Help me carry this stuff inside, will you?"

He shook his head. "Leave it." He tucked her left hand into his right arm. "I'll send a couple guys out to get it. You—" The way he effortlessly led her toward the door to the restaurant, you couldn't tell that he was nearly dragging her. "I want to show you something."

Reilly gave up and merely dragged her feet. "Does it involve your staff?"

He chuckled warmly. "Only if you want it to."

"SOMEBODY'S BEEN tampering with our orders."

The instant Ben and Reilly had entered the back of the restaurant, Lance had descended. "Explain 'tampering.'"

Lance tapped a pad he was holding. "Simple. Somebody—outside—has been accessing our orders via the Internet and changing them with our suppliers. At first I thought it might be someone here, but I got a hold of a friend of mine at the brewery who knows his way around a computer and he said that the Tia Maria order that was changed was done from a remote terminal with no footprints, not from his computer or ours.''

Ben had to tear his gaze away from where Reilly had wandered into the restaurant proper. ''Interesting. Do you have any idea who would do that?''

''Nope. I was hoping that's where you would come in.''

He didn't have a clue who would want to do something like that.

''At any rate, I have an understanding with our suppliers that they're to print out our orders the instant they receive them and that they stand as initially put through unless they hear directly from us with an invoice number.'' He tucked the pad under his arm, following Ben's gaze to Reilly. ''Who's the lady?''

Ben blinked at him. ''Ask me again later.''

Lance held up his hands. ''Hey, you don't have to ask me twice to leave you alone.'' He grinned. ''I'll be out back.''

After Lance made a silent exit, Ben stood back and watched Reilly walk through his restaurant, his one obsession, his pride and joy. The only thing in his life that had meant anything to him for so long—outside his father—that it felt unusual to want her to like it. To want Reilly to approve.

She seemed to look with her fingers, running them along the smooth line of the bar, the fine wood of the tables, over the silk of the red and gold tablecloths. Vintage posters of 30s and 40s movies hung on the roughhewn wood walls, multicolored crystal beads draped around them. Mini-electric lamps with fringed, red velvet shades sat in the middle of each table. The decor had changed over the years, but he'd always stuck to a 30s prohibition era theme. A true hideaway from the world outside.

All but for the wall of glass at the other side of the restaurant that offered up a panoramic view of the Pacific.

Reilly came to a stop at the glass. And Ben's gaze had never left her profile as he slowly followed her through the place. His place.

"It's breathtaking," she whispered, hugging her arms around herself.

He nodded. "It is, isn't it? I remember going there," he said, pointing to a spot at the bottom of the cliff, "to fish with my father when I was kid every Sunday morning. Back then, this place was little more than an abandoned fishing shack. I used to spend my time looking up at it, dreaming, thinking of all the things I'd like to do with it."

He felt her gaze on him. "You always wanted to open a restaurant?"

He looked at her. "No. First I envisioned this ultimate skateboarders heaven. It was at the beginning of the extreme sports turn. The only problem was my dad wouldn't let me have a skateboard, so that dream vanished pretty quickly." He chuckled. "I lost a lot of fish that way. My dad said that I'd miss out on a lot of opportunities in life if I kept walking around with my head in the clouds."

"And your mom?"

He slid his hands into the pockets of his slacks and squinted out at the waves just beginning to throw back the morning sun. "Never knew her. She left my dad shortly after I was born."

"Oh, God, I'm sorry."

He scanned her pretty face, ascertaining that she genuinely was. Having met so many people over the years he'd owned the restaurant, he knew that people always said the words, but not many of them meant it.

Not that he went around telling everyone about his mother. He didn't. In fact, he was surprised he'd shared what he had with Reilly. Actually, a lot of what he did with Reilly surprised him. He'd never come on to a woman as strongly as he did her. And the teasing...

"What about you?" he asked.

"Me?"

"Family? Mother and father?"

"Big one. I'm the middle of five children. Mom and Dad are still together."

She seemed to hesitate over something, then closed her delectable mouth.

"This place is everything and far more than I even imagined it would be. And I have quite an active imagination," she murmured, turning to look out the window again. "Your dad must be proud."

Ben stepped over to the bar and let himself behind

it. "I don't know how he would feel. He's never been here."

"Never?"

He shook his head as he went about making a strong pot of coffee.

"Does he live far away?"

"Same spot we've always lived." He pointed down the beach. "About a mile down that way in an old apartment complex."

"So why…" her words drifted off. "Never mind. I'm being nosy, aren't I?"

He blinked at her. "No. You're being human." More human than anyone he'd met in a long, long time.

When was the last time someone asked him about his family? His father? And not only listened but asked follow-up questions? Too often he encountered people who used questions to launch into their own life's story. But not Reilly.

"You say that like you don't know many of them." She climbed up on top of a bar stool across from him. "Humans, I mean."

He took two cups out of a dishwasher. "Maybe it's because I don't."

She seemed to consider him for a long time, then said, "Well maybe it's long past time you met more."

Ben was getting the strong impression that he already had. With Reilly.

He told her about his father owning three hot-dog stands. About how his father felt about his selling those stands and buying this place. About how the older man felt he wouldn't fit in if he did come.

The words flowed out of his mouth easily, unchecked, and Reilly seemed to take every last one of them in.

"Every Friday morning I call to invite him. And every Friday he tells me, no, he's got something else to do," he finished up, placing a cup in front of her and staying right where he was on the opposite side of the bar.

Truth was, he liked this. Liked talking to Reilly in a way that felt...cathartic somehow. Like what he said mattered to her simply because it mattered to him. And he knew if he was sitting next to her he wouldn't be able to squash the need to touch her, chase away all conversation.

She slowly sipped her coffee, leaving untouched the sugar and fresh cream he'd put out. "Invite him on a Monday then."

The suggestion was so simple, so straightforward, that Ben didn't immediately know how to react. Of course. All along he'd wanted his father to come on his busiest night, perhaps needing to show him how successful the business was. He'd never thought that the crowded environment might be the very reason his father stayed away.

Reilly was looking around again. "I can't see him not liking the place, Ben. I mean, it's so... comfortable. The hideaway thing really works. I imagine that if you're sitting in one of those booths you feel buffeted from the world for a short, precious time.''

He dropped his gaze to her full, unpainted mouth. Took in the natural honey glow of her skin. She was such a breath of fresh air. She appealed to him on so many levels that he would probably be more than a bit…concerned had it been anyone else. But for some reason he couldn't define, he felt he could trust her. And it had been so long since he'd let go of the reins, he had a hard time keeping from reaching for them again.

Then he'd looked into her eyes and felt a response that was so rare, so unusual that he couldn't help but give himself over to it. And he'd kissed her and wanted her with a potency that made him forget not only about those damn reins, but everything else along with it.

He wanted this woman. With an intensity that far surpassed anything a physical meeting would provide.

He also suspected that if she knew what he was thinking, she'd run full-out in the opposite direction.

''You're coming to dinner Wednesday night?'' he asked, not wanting to push her. Not wanting to scare her off, but still needing on some deep level to get her to commit, even if it was only to a dinner date.

She stared down into her coffee, avoiding his attempts at eye contact. He caught the tightening of her fingers against the white cup. The stiffening of her shoulders. And he knew that she wanted to refuse his invitation. Wanted to keep the distance between them

that he felt lessening each moment they spent together.

Then he watched everything relax as she sat back
and smiled at him. "I'd love to."

7

If she was supposed to be going to dinner at Benardo's in two day's time, what was Ben doing knocking at her door at ten o'clock that same night?

Reilly jerked away from where she could see his handsome face through the peephole of her apartment door then flattened her back against the wood. No doubt about it. Ben was standing on the iron landing waiting for her to answer. And since she'd yelled out, "Coming," thinking it might be Layla—who was known to stop by every now and again on her way home from the clinic—or Mallory, who occasionally came by to raid her kitchen—or even one of her nieces, she had little choice but to confront him.

She looked around her apartment. Shabby chic didn't come close to describing her surroundings. Especially with pastry cookbooks open all over the coffee table and notepads with ideas on recipe variations on top of them, and a rerun of *Friends* on TV.

What was he doing here?

She looked down at her T-shirt and panties, then turned to open the door a crack. "Ben! What are you doing here?"

He held up a bag. "I was in the neighborhood and

thought I'd give you a preview of what will be on the menu Wednesday night.''

Reilly felt stupidly pleased that he'd thought of her. ''Um, give me a minute. I need to put something on.''

''Oh, no need to do so on my account.''

She slammed the door in his face then ran for the bedroom. Now the dilemma lay in what she should wear.

She settled on a simple pair of jean shorts. After a quick check of herself in the mirror, wiping at a smudge here, fluffing her hair there, she crossed back to the door. Only when she had it open did she realize she didn't have a bra on under her T-shirt. And that Ben not only noticed the oversight, but had his gaze glued right there, where her nipples were hard and pushing against the soft fabric.

''Come in,'' she said, hunching her shoulders as far as she could without looking like the Hunchback of Notre Dame. ''I'll be, um, right back.''

She went back to her bedroom, started rifling around in her drawer for the red bra she'd bought a long time ago but rarely wore, only realizing as she began to take off her T-shirt that Ben was watching her through the open door.

''Perv,'' she said, closing the door on his chuckle.

A minute later she came back out, having lightly spritzed on some kind of pink powdery perfume Efi had left there last Saturday and quickly brushing her teeth.

If it was in the back of her mind that she might get laid tonight, she wasn't going to dwell on it.

Ben was still standing where she'd left him. He lifted the bag. ''Where do you want this?''

She cleared her throat, realizing he couldn't sit down because there was nowhere to sit. Not with the cookbooks littering the joint. ''Put it in the kitchen.'' When he turned to do that, she quickly straightened the place up, piling the cookbooks on top of one another while trying not to lose her places. ''Actually, while what's in there smells great, I'm not very hungry. So unless you haven't eaten—''

Her breath froze in her lungs when she found him standing in the kitchen doorway, looking magnificent. He had rolled up the sleeves of his dress shirt. His arms were folded over his huge chest and his feet were crossed at the ankles. ''I ate something at the restaurant earlier.''

She fluffed a couple of pillows, became aware that she had her bottom to him, probably waving it at him like a red flag to a bull, and repositioned herself. ''You want to grab a couple of beers, then?''

She heard the refrigerator open and close then he was handing her a cold bottle. She held it up as if to salute him then took a small swig.

The sound of tinny laughter filled the apartment and she reached for the remote to turn off the TV.

''Don't,'' Ben said quietly. ''I watch *Friends* almost every night.''

''You do?'' she asked, surprised and not knowing

why she was surprised. "Of course you do. A lot of people do. Or else they wouldn't put it on. Right?"

She was babbling again. God, what was wrong with her? It seemed every time she saw him she made a fool out of herself. First by hiding in the kitchen at the shop. Then by hiding in her van that morning. And now by yakking away like her fifteen-year-old niece.

"Please...sit."

He gave her one of those closed-mouth smiles that drove her insane with the desire to kiss him. Made her itch to pry those delicious lips open with her tongue and have at the humor and charm that oozed from him like a cologne. Which seemed only natural because she couldn't seem to detect cologne on him. A definite change in scenery because most men seemed to bathe in the stuff. Cologne should definitely come with a warning label: less is more. Then again, if they didn't go through it so quickly, then they wouldn't buy as much, so that pretty much defeated the business purpose, didn't it?

Reilly cringed, realizing that she was now mentally babbling.

"You're nervous, aren't you?" Ben asked.

She stared at him. Yes. "No."

"Would it help if we got some things out of the way first?"

"Things? What things?"

He gripped the bottle she held. She resisted the urge to fight him for it, to keep holding it so she would have something to do with her hands, although she had no intention of drinking it. Do you know how many calories even twelve ounces of light beer has in it?

"Things like this…"

And just like that he was kissing her.

Dear Lord, he was kissing her.

Reilly felt her muscles go limp, her body automatically curving into his, primordially seeking what she mentally had been denying it. Oh, he felt so good pressed against her. She loved the way her softness rasped against his hardness. Adored the way he threaded his fingers through her hair then let them rest against the nape of her neck, teasing the skin there. When he was kissing her it was all too easy to believe that they were equals, meeting on common ground, not two people from different sides of the social spectrum. While he'd probably always been a part of the "in" crowd, she had been the person the "innies" had targeted for bullying. She hadn't gone to one of her school dances. Had always sat at the back of the class, hoping against hope she could disappear. And while their time together at the restaurant earlier had erased some very important lines between them, she knew they could be no more than friends, because a girl formerly known as Chubby Chuddy had absolutely zero future possibilities with hot, popular and sexy Ben Kane.

He slipped his tongue into her mouth, the hand at the back of her neck sliding down over her back and down to her bottom. She groaned, giving herself over to the hot, hot desire washing over her. She pressed her palms against his chest through his crisp Egyptian broadcloth shirt. Oh, the hell with tomorrow. Why worry about that when today was turning out so, so well?

He pulled back slightly and gave her a couple of wet, juicy closed-mouth kisses. "Better?" he asked with a grin, very little of his blue irises recognizable beyond his dilated pupils.

"Hmm?"

"I asked if you were feeling better. You know, if your nervousness is gone." His fingers swept over the back of her thigh where her shorts ended and her hypersensitized bare skin began.

"That's what you meant by getting some things out of the way first?" she managed to push through her tight throat. She could feel his hard arousal pressing against her stomach and shivered. "Kissing me?"

"Mmm. Seems you always relax when we kiss."

Did she?

Yes, she realized, she did.

"So that's the extent of the…things?" she asked, tilting her head cockily to the side.

He watched the move, his gaze skimming over her exposed neck, down the front of her T-shirt then down to her jean shorts. She idly wondered if he was considering what kind of underwear she had on.

"Yes," he said, his gaze slamming back into hers.

Reilly was wholly disappointed.

"Oh, don't get me wrong. I fully intend to have sex with you tonight, Reilly." His grin was decidedly salacious. "I just thought we'd sit and watch the sitcom first."

She considered him and what he was saying and then everything that had happened since she found him standing outside her door. He struck her as the type of man who, when he wanted something, took it. Why, then, was he taking his time now?

"Screw the sitcom," she said, yanking his shirt from his slacks and making for his zipper.

He held her hips firmly and chuckled. "I was hoping you'd say that. After all, there's only so much a man can take...."

IF ONLY BEN had known that comment would extend to different areas of his expanding relationship with Reilly. Before he could blink, she'd essentially ripped off his clothes, pulled her T-shirt over her head to reveal the red bra he'd seen her take out of her drawer earlier, then shimmied out of her decadent little jean cutoffs. He took in the sexy little black satin bikini underwear and knew a pang of disappointment. Where were the mammoth underpants?

She pushed him to the couch then straddled him, her blond hair mussed from where he'd run his fingers through it, her lips full and pouty and her body primed and more than ready.

"Who knew you'd be such a wildcat?" he murmured, catching her head and holding her still for a precious moment so he could look at her. Her hazel eyes twinkled, amusement and a hint of a challenge in them.

"I'm a woman into extremes. When I do something, I go all the way." She wore a determined expression. "What's the matter, Ben? Afraid you can't handle a woman like me?"

What would the equivalent to Dr. Jekyll and Mr. Hyde be? Miss Hyde? Ms. Hyde? The Reilly he was presented with now was so different from the self-conscious, hesitant woman he thought he was coming to know that he had to take another look to make sure it was the same person.

And the contrast turned him on to no end.

"Not the case at all, Reilly. I just want to know where the fire is."

She curved her fingers around his wrist then tugged his hand down until his fingers rested against the front of her panties. "Right here," she whispered. She tucked his fingers inside the waistband and shuddered as his fingertips made contact with her springy curls then burrowed beyond them to the swollen flesh beyond.

"Oh, yes," she whispered, her eyes fluttering closed as she stretched her neck back.

And he thought he was hot. She was very definitely burning up. And the knowledge that it was for him affected him on a fundamental level that notched his need up even further.

He had the distinct feeling that with Reilly there

would never be any complaints like "you're on my hair." Or "my arm's falling asleep." Or "I have a headache." She seemed to run on some sort of unseen energy source that caught him up in the firestorm. He could only watch, amazed, as she got up again, slipped out of her panties, then climbed back on top of him again, gloriously unconcerned that she was naked in the full light from a nearby lamp.

"Condom," she rasped.

Ben reached for his pants and pulled one of out of his back pocket. She took it from him and ripped open the packet with her straight, even teeth, then seemed to consider his length and width before carefully sheathing him.

Ben gritted his back teeth together at the sensation of cool latex and hot fingers against his pulsing erection. Then she was grabbing the back of the sofa on either side of his head and sinking down, taking him in, slowly, inch by precious inch.

So tight…so slick…so hot.

When she'd taken the last of him inside, she took a shuddering breath, her eyes closed, her tongue restlessly licking her full lips. Ben was mesmerized by the enraptured expression on her pretty face. An expression he didn't think he'd seen another woman wear without the help of drugs or alcohol. No, Reilly was high on pure sex.

He grazed his hands down her sides then around to pop the catch on her bra. The satiny fabric gave like a rubber band, sliding halfway down her arms. Reilly didn't seem to notice as she slowly rose from his shaft then sank back down again, obviously reveling in the feel of him filling her. He rasped his palms over her taut nipples then leaned forward to pull one deep into his mouth. Her slick muscles convulsed around him and he threw his head back and groaned.

Up and down…up and down… Reilly moved, each move faster than the one before, causing her breasts to jiggle enticingly, her cheeks reddening from the activity. Her firm bottom met with his upper thighs then lifted again until she was virtually bouncing on top of him, her breathing faster, a long moan exiting her sexy mouth.

An incredible climax was building in Ben's balls. Accumulating and swirling and threatening to erupt each time her smooth skin slapped against his. He grasped her hips to try to slow her movements but she pried his fingers from her flesh and quickened the pace even further. He watched her face, seeing determination there. Passion. Ecstasy. And a single-minded desire to find what she was looking for as fast as she could.

And Ben was helpless to stop her.

He rested his head back against the sofa, hoping he wouldn't lose it before she reached orgasm. But it was growing more and more difficult to hold off with her delectable breasts swaying in front of him, her engorged womanhood sinking down to cover him, lubricating him with her thick juices, her face just as rapturous as any on a porno magazine cover. Sweat ran down her cheek, capturing strands of her hair there as her moans grew deeper and longer.

''Oh, yes,'' she whispered as he held on for dear life. ''Oh, yes, yes, yes.''

He vaguely recalled her asking him if he was afraid she was too much woman for him. As he watched her climb to the top of sensation mountain and launch herself off, and then chased right over the other side with her, he wondered if she hadn't been too far from the truth. Maybe Reilly *was* way too much woman for him.

8

TWO DAYS LATER Reilly stood in front of the mirror at the bridal shop, her own wistful sigh filling her ears. She caught herself and checked to make sure Mallory hadn't noticed. God, she'd never hear the end of it if Mallory even caught an inkling that she and Ben had…well, that he had come over and…

She smiled so wide she was afraid she'd pull a facial muscle.

She and Ben had glorious, all night long, hot, sweaty, totally orgasmic sex.

When she'd finally begun to drift off to sleep in his arms at somewhere around two Tuesday morning, she'd been half-afraid, and half-hopeful that he wouldn't be there in the morning. Instead, he'd kissed her temple so sweetly her heart had ached and told her he needed to get back home, they both had early mornings. She'd nodded and lain snuggled there in the sheets that smelled like the time they'd spent together and drifted off to sleep when it might have been a good idea to follow him out and make sure the door was locked after him.

Now she cleared her throat, her gaze dropping to the pink taffeta dress. Definitely not the image that went along with her thoughts. Definitely not a choice that would be made by a woman capable of rational thought.

She resisted the urge to act like she was choking herself with her finger as she met Mallory's equally disgusted look in the mirror where she stood behind her.

"Oh, they're beautiful!" Layla gushed, coming in wearing a creamy silk robe and looking them over. "And they're the type of dresses you can wear anywhere, you know, after the ceremony."

Mallory gave Layla a long look. "Sure, if some desperate high school senior with bad acne asks me to the prom."

Layla blinked at her as the seamstress yanked on the zipper on the side of Reilly's dress.

"They're fine, Layla," Reilly rushed to reassure her friend. "Ignore her. You know Mallory turns into a jagged-toothed monster whenever she has to take off one of her repulsive T-shirts."

They all looked to where Mallory actually still had today's T-shirt on under her dress. You could make out the words "You" and "Bitch." Reilly knew from having read it earlier that it said: You Call Me a Bitch Like It's an Insult.

Reilly still didn't have a clue where she bought all these offensive shirts. All she knew was that she rarely saw her friend wear the same one twice.

The seamstress yanked on the zipper, nearly pulling

Reilly off the high heels she would be wearing with the dress. "Are you sure you're a size eight?"

Reilly stared at her in the mirror. "A perfect size eight."

The seamstress gave another yank then sat back on her heels and sighed. "Yes, well, I think we'd better try a perfect size nine."

Reilly blinked as if unable to translate her words. She'd been the same weight for the past nine years. It was impossible that she'd gained even an ounce. And it wasn't anywhere near that time of the month, so that couldn't be to blame.

Mallory elbowed her to move from in front of the mirror. "So you've gained a couple of pounds. So what? My weight fluctuates five pounds all the time." She met her gaze in the mirror. "You know, depending on whether I'm dating a hot guy who's great in the sack or not."

Reilly didn't really hear her as she stumbled backward and plopped down on the chair against the wall. She absently noticed the way Layla glared at Mallory, but couldn't bring herself to respond. If a great sack session made a difference in weight, then she should have lost a good three pounds the other night with Ben.

Instead she had gained weight.

"My jeans still fit."

"That's because you wear them too big to begin with," Mallory pointed out.

"Mall," Layla said in warning.

Mallory blinked at her. "Why are you staring at me like I just backed over your dog, Lay? For God's sake, I'm going to wear this hideous thing for you, aren't I?"

"Hideous?" Layla repeated, an ominous edge to her usually controlled voice.

The seamstress stepped in front of Reilly. "Shall I get the nine?"

"No!" Layla and Reilly said in unison while Mallory rolled her eyes in the mirror.

"I'll...just have to lose a few pounds before the ceremony," Reilly said, kicking off the shoes then getting up to get out of the dress.

"Five."

She stared at the seamstress.

"You'll have to lose at least five. All around the middle."

Reilly felt the ridiculous urge to sock her. Didn't the size zero woman who could probably eat an entire cow and not gain a pound know that she'd spent her childhood as Chubby Chuddy? Didn't she understand that keeping a size eight was an obsession with her? That she owned a pastry shop and never indulged in the pastries.

She thought back on the past week and groaned. Well, she usually didn't indulge in the pastries. But she'd caught herself on several occasions chewing on a random sticky bun or cream horn, more than a little distracted by thoughts of Ben Kane.

Oh, she so knew that getting involved with him wasn't a good idea.

Most women lost weight while having great sex.

She gained it.

So rationally speaking, if they continued seeing each other, she stood to gain back every ounce of the weight she'd lost nine years ago.

Now she wanted to sock herself. What a ridiculous notion, Ben Kane's being to blame for her weight gain. Although she suspected it was easier to point the finger at him than at herself. If her childhood had taught her anything it was that she wasn't very good at moderation. It was all or nothing. She couldn't just have one sticky bun, she had to have three.

One night with Ben wasn't enough, she had to have as many as she possibly could.

And in both cases, she was more than a little reckless when it came to considering the consequences.

"I'll start running again," she said, pulling on her jeans. She stared at the denim, swearing that they'd gotten tighter just since taking them off ten minutes ago. "That's it. I'll start running again."

"When?" Mallory asked, fitting perfectly into her size six. "Oh, wait a minute. You could do it before you start baking at 3:00 a.m. Then there's always midnight when you knock off work." Her face lit up. "Hey, I've got an idea. Layla's marrying the talented Dr. Sam Lovejoy," she said, drawing out his last name. "Plastic surgeon to the stars. Maybe he can do some lipo or something."

"Shut up, Mall," Layla said.

"Sit-ups," the seamstress said. "Or two hours of yoga every morning. Maybe both."

Mallory, who was ignoring Layla, made a face at the young woman. "Yeah, who needs sleep anyway?"

"Sex," Layla said.

Reilly nearly choked on her own saliva.

"What?" her blond friend asked. "I'm marrying the guy. I'm allowed."

Reilly pretended interest in the dress she'd just taken off, checking to make sure it was the size the seamstress said it was. What she was really doing was ignoring Mallory's inquisitive gaze.

"So where's the dress?" she asked Layla in a desperate attempt to budge the subject from sex.

She watched as her friend plopped down in the chair she'd just vacated. "I haven't decided yet."

"I thought you were going with the off-the-shoulder one? You have great shoulders," Mallory said, telling the seamstress where to take her dress in.

Reilly felt an irrational desire to lift the skirt and strangle the woman with it.

"The ceremony's in December, Mall. While it's still warm here, it's not *that* warm. Especially not when the reception is at night in my father's backyard."

What went without saying was that three humongous tents were going to be erected for the event and that Layla's stepmother was checking into space heaters as they spoke even though southern California rarely dipped below the mid-fifties at night.

Reilly pretended to fix her hair in the mirror when what she was really doing was checking her body for telltale bulges. Had Ben noticed anything the other night? Not that he had anything to compare her current weight to, but surely he had to realize she wasn't the rail-thin model type he was so used to seeing. Did he think her a horse?

"You're awfully quiet, Rei," Mallory said.

Her friend had changed out of her own bridesmaid dress and in the mirror the words across her T-shirt looked stranger yet. "Just tired, that's all," she said.

"And have you, um, heard from Ben Kane lately?"

She looked to Layla for help but instead found her looking at her curiously, as well.

"Actually," she said carefully, "I've agreed to go to dinner at his restaurant tonight."

Dinner. She could handle it. She just wouldn't eat anything, that's all. She was used to doing that. Did it every time she went to her parents' house for an occasional Sunday dinner. Had turned into an expert at refilling her water glass and picking at her dressingless salad. She'd learned quickly that after the first five minutes of "eat up, Reilly," everyone usually forgot to pay attention to what she was or wasn't eating. And so long as she piled the leftover food up just so to look like she'd eaten her fill, no one noticed afterward, either.

Vitamins. She'd have to pick up some more after

she left the bridal shop. And liquid proteins. She had five pounds to lose and she intended to do it as soon as humanly possible.

"OPEN."

Okay, her plan not to eat anything at Ben's restaurant wasn't working. Simply because she'd forgotten his little habit of wanting to feed her.

It might be a Wednesday night, but the place was filled to capacity, her and Ben sitting in a corner booth, buffeted from the remaining diners by red beads draped around the upper part of the booth. She hadn't known what to expect. Maybe a small cutting board for two in the kitchen. But when Ben had immediately spotted her in the front doorway, he'd whisked her to the best seat in the house and proceeded to order what seemed like everything on the menu.

"Open," Ben said again, waving the overloaded forkful of stuffed mushroom in front of her nose.

Oh, it smelled so good.

Oh, she was such a hog.

She tried to take a small bite off the end of the mushroom but Ben took advantage of her open mouth and shoved the entire fork inside.

Was he trying to fatten her up?

The appetizer melted on her tongue and she couldn't help closing her eyes and moaning. Damn, but it tasted so good.

"What do you think?" Ben's soft voice made her eyelids flutter back open.

It was clear that he enjoyed feeding her. His pupils dilated and his gaze was so focused on her that she suspected an earthquake could shake the ground beneath them and he would probably think nothing of it.

"Heavenly."

He grinned. "I made it."

She raised her brows. Not only did the guy enjoy feeding her, he'd made the food himself. "No kidding?"

"No kidding."

She gestured toward the desserts on the end of the table. "I have to tell you, I'm not going to touch any of that."

He was turning the plate around in front of him, probably choosing the next thing he intended to feed her. "Why? Are you dieting?"

Reilly nearly choked on the water she was gulping down in an effort to fill her rumbling stomach. "Doesn't everyone?"

"In my opinion, you need to put on a few more pounds."

What? This from the man who had dated every supermodel this side of the Atlantic?

He waggled his brows at her. "A man doesn't like to get bruised when things get hot and sticky, if you know what I mean."

Unfortunately she did. And she found that she'd

like to do some more of the hot and sticky stuff right then.

"Open."

She eyed the octopus on the end of the fork. Now this she could easily say she didn't eat. "Sorry. I don't do octopus."

"You'll like this."

She shook her head again. No matter how delicious, the eight-legged bottom feeder wasn't worth the calories she'd be putting on her hips. "Go for something else." She reached for her own fork. "In fact, I think I'm capable of feeding myself from here on out."

"Oh."

Ben looked so disappointed that she nearly tucked the linen napkin inside the top of her black dress and told him to have at it. Eating the entire contents of the table would be worth it if only it would wipe away that expression.

His grin made a quick return. "And here I was having so much fun."

She settled in a little more comfortably across the table from him now that she had control of the fork firmly back in her court. "So tell me, is the place always this crowded?"

She pretended to eat a piece of green lettuce as he looked around, seeming surprised to discover where they were. "It didn't use to be. In the beginning barely half the tables would fill up."

"And now you're all the rage."

He crossed his arms on top of the table. "Hollywood's a bit fickle."

"But you've managed to maintain a pretty steady reputation."

"I'm doing all right."

All right? From where she sat he was doing phenomenally well. You couldn't open a magazine or a newspaper without seeing Benardo's Hideaway mentioned somewhere. Either by stars that had been photographed leaving the restaurant or by food critics who raved about the cuisine.

He looked up from where he'd been contemplating the table. "By the way, I talked to my father today. I did what you suggested and invited him to dinner next Monday."

Reilly realized she had shoveled a good portion of a stuffed mushroom into her mouth and stopped chewing. "And?"

Ben's blue eyes sparkled. "He's coming."

Reilly quickly smiled and reached for his hand. "Oh, Ben, that's great!"

"Of course, he requested that I have a special kind of beer on hand that isn't on the menu."

"Something imported?"

"Something cheap."

She laughed. "So you make him happy. What's the big deal?"

He shook his head. "With his request? Nothing. But...I don't know. I've had the doors to the place open for seven years and he decides to come now. I don't get it. It has to be more than just the day of the week.''

Reilly looked over the place. He had a point. She guessed that Benardo's was busy every night of the week.

"I've also been wondering how I'll react if he hates the place.''

"How could he possibly hate it?'' she asked, forcing herself to put her hands in her lap before she demolished the contents of every plate in front of her then used the bread to mop up whatever gravy, sauce or oil remained.

Ben shrugged and leaned back. "I don't know. It's not one of his hot-dog stands, I guess.''

"Do you have hot dogs on the menu?''

He chuckled good-naturedly. "No.''

"Maybe you should think about adding one hot dog type plate to the lunch menu.''

He looked thoughtful for a minute.

"Not anything cheesy. Something a little more upscale with special toppings. Like black beans—they appear to be popular now although I could do without them, thank you. Different cheeses. And you could use some kind of sausage, like kielbasa. You know. Something more gourmet, but when it comes down to it it's really just a hot dog under all the toppings.''

He seemed to be looking at her a little too closely. Reilly resisted the urge to ask if she had something on her face. A bit of spinach between her teeth, even though she was pretty sure that's not what was on Ben's mind.

"What?" she couldn't help herself from asking as she fidgeted in the comfortable leather booth.

"You could be making a comment on people with that statement," he said quietly.

"What? That we're all hot dogs underneath our toppings?"

He smiled as he turned her hand over and drew his fingertips along the ultrasensitive skin there. She tried to suppress a shiver, but failed, tilting her head when it raced up her spine and neck.

"No. That when you take away all the trappings, the games, we're all just human."

"Hmm. Seems to be a frequent topic with us. Humanity."

He pressed his lips against her palm. "Yes, it does, doesn't it?"

She fought to concentrate on the mental path he was leading her down, but her body battled back, much happier focusing on the flick of his tongue against her skin, the wholly provocative expression on his face, and the suggestion in his eyes that they could be doing something much, much more interesting in that one moment.

She restlessly licked her lips. "I, um, guess we all get so wrapped up in the busyness of our own lives that we don't take much time out to consider life as a whole. I mean…what does it all mean, anyway?" Her heart thrummed an erratic rhythm in her chest as he trailed the very tip of his forefinger down her wrist and up her arm to her elbow.

Oh boy.

"You're the only one who's made me stop to think about it," Ben murmured, his attention on her skin.

If he didn't stop, she was going to slide down under the table and pull him along with her.

The lights flickered. Reilly couldn't be sure if it was reality or an extension of her own short-circuiting brain. But then the lights went out altogether, leaving only the light of the setting sun filtering in through the windows and a quiet hush hanging over the room.

"Damn," Ben muttered, seeming reluctant to let her go.

Yep. Those were her sentiments exactly as she watched him scoot from the booth and start for the back of the restaurant, leaving Reilly alone to ponder his words, his mouth, her own lack of control when it came to him and food, and the restlessness of the customers around her.

As she sat quietly in the dark, she wondered what the future held for her and Ben Kane. Was it just her, or did things seemed to be getting serious fast? Or was she an ingenue when it came to the dating scene and that what was passing between them was normal first-time dating stuff? She couldn't be sure. But she did know she wanted—no, longed for—it to continue. Even as a part of her worried about what would happen when Ben would eventually wake up and see her for who she really was and bolt in the other direction.

She wouldn't think about that now. Couldn't think about that now.

In fact, she decided she needed to do something other than sit there in the dark before she turned into an emotional basket case altogether.

Either that or eat all the delicious-smelling food on the table in front of her under the cover of darkness.

She slid from the booth, firmly deciding on the former. She'd never fit into that bridesmaid dress if she did the latter.

9

THE POWER OUTAGE was just one in a long line of mysterious mishaps in the past week, testing Ben's patience. And why this one had to happen tonight of all nights further agitated him. In the kitchen, he consulted with Lance, propping open the doors to both the dining area and the back so at least a little light penetrated the complete darkness. The quiet hum of conversation between the guests was starting to get a little louder, a little more anxious.

Lance was running his hands through his hair. "I don't know what's going on, boss. The outage isn't local. I checked the fuse box and looked outside, but couldn't find any sign of the cause."

Great. In the seven years since opening the restaurant, he'd never encountered a power outage before.

"Candles."

Ben turned to find Reilly behind him.

"Surely, you have candles around here someplace? Get them and have the servers put one on each of the tables. Two, if you have enough. And line them up along the bar in front of the mirrors to reflect the light."

In fact, they did have candles. A lot of them they'd

accumulated for the summer when the dining area extended to the deck overlooking the beach and for Valentine's Day every year.

Ben set out to order the servers to do just that, when Reilly touched his arm.

"No, Lance can do that. You need to go out and soothe your guests. Throw them a freebie. Make the happening seem like something unexpectedly... romantic."

Ben gazed down into her shadowy face. God, but he was coming to...like this woman. A lot. She was quick on her feet. Inventive. In control. And sexier than all get out.

"Gotcha, boss," he said to her with a grin.

He noticed the way her chin dipped down to her chest and wished he could see her blush.

He went out to give a general announcement to the diners, then moved from table to table, personally addressing each guest and reassuring them that dinner would be served as usual. As he did so, he noticed that Reilly had tied a server's apron around her waist, covering her sexy black dress, and was helping set out the candles with a warm and friendly smile. Just seeing her made him feel less worried, more at ease. And made him want her all the more.

When he made his way back to the kitchen twenty minutes later, he found Reilly talking to Lance in the light of dozens of candles placed carefully around the room. "You work with gas stoves, right?" she was saying. "We need appetizers. A lot of them. Oh, and drinks! Make sure everyone's glass is kept full."

Ben came up behind her, brushing suggestively against her backside in her form-fitting dress. He caught her shiver.

"What's the status on the outage?" he asked Lance over Reilly's shoulder.

"Edison said they can't send anyone out until morning. I'm waiting to hear back from a private electrician now. Through his wife, I promised him double his usual take if he can make it here tonight."

"Good."

"Does anyone play piano?" Reilly asked the kitchen staff.

Piano?

"I do. Some," one of his newer servers said quietly.

"Come here," Reilly motioned toward the young blonde. She told her to turn around, helped her take off her apron, pulled her white blouse out of her slacks then tied the ends around the young woman's slender stomach. She turned her back around and pulled her hair out of her ponytail and fluffed it around her head. "Go. Keep it low and soft, but upbeat."

The girl seemed shocked.

"I'll double your pay for the night," Ben added.

"You don't have to say that twice," the girl said and darted out of the kitchen.

To look at Reilly's face you wouldn't know that

she'd just backed up against him, discreetly rubbing her bottom against the front of his slacks. But, oh, did Ben ever know it. "Nice move, that one," she whispered.

"You took the words right out of my mouth."

THREE HOURS LATER, while kissing Reilly, Ben opened the door to what he called his bungalow, but what was really a sprawling one-story house, situated a quarter mile up from the restaurant and perched on a cliff. He backed her into the dark living room, tugging at the straps of her dress as he went.

She tasted good. Add to that the fact that she had essentially saved the night from complete ruin at the restaurant and he was suitably in awe of her. Was there anything this woman couldn't do?

He fumbled to turn on the lights, rotating the dimmer to low even as she pushed his shirt down over his arms, not completing the task before she dove for the front of his slacks. He shook his arms one by one to free himself of the thick cotton.

He chuckled softly, sliding the straps of her dress down over her arms and leaving them there, essentially trapping her in the same way she had unwittingly trapped him moments before.

She drew slightly away, her breath coming in ragged gasps as she stared up at him, her hazel eyes all light and warmth and passion.

"You're an impatient one, aren't you?" he whispered, bending to kiss the curve of her sweet-smelling neck then skimming his mouth up over her delicate jawline.

"Hot. I'm hot."

He looked down at her. "Oh, I already know that, Reilly."

She struggled to free herself of her makeshift bindings.

"Not so fast. We did it your way last time. Now it's time we gave my way a chance."

"Your…way?" she whispered so low he nearly didn't make out her words.

"Mmm-hmm."

He watched her swallow with apparent difficulty.

"Nice and slow…"

She slid her leg between his and drew her knee up to rub against his crotch. "Slow's overrated."

"Don't knock it until you've tried it."

"I have—"

He claimed her mouth to keep the words from coming out. "Not with me, you haven't."

Thankfully she had no response to that one except the heaving of her chest as she fought for air.

He swept her up into his arms and carried her to his bedroom at the back of the house overlooking the sea. The view wasn't that different than the restaurant's. The important difference, however, being the king-size bed situated in the middle of the room covered in black silk and a thick black-patterned comforter. He pushed the remote to open the sheer curtains, then pushed another button that opened the windows entirely. While a bit on the chilly side, the fresh, invigorating smell of the ocean air created an atmosphere he had been waiting all night to show her.

Reilly gasped, staring at the way the bright moonlight shimmered off the white-topped waves some fifty feet below the cliff then stretched off in a silvery line that seemed to pave the way to forever. She took a deep breath of the salty Pacific. All at once she seemed to forget about her restless urgency. Judging her readiness for him to take the lead, Ben laid her across the bed and skimmed her dress down and off, revealing two scraps of silk and lace that were her panties and bra. He again knew a moment of disappointment that she wasn't wearing the enormous underwear that still played such a large role in his private fantasies.

He took in her face in the dim moonlight. Her eyes were big and luminescent. Her lips plump and parted. Her glorious hair tousled and appealing. Damn, but she was beautiful.

He ran his hands slowly down her sides, content for now to skim over her undergarments. But on the second pass he did away with both, baring her to his gaze. Every part of her was in perfect proportion with the next. Her breasts were just the right size. Her nipples perfect for her breasts. Her waist not too narrow. Her hips full and soft. The golden triangle of hair between her legs trimmed just so, but not overly done.

He parted her thighs and she slowly opened to him, revealing the pink engorged flesh that lay waiting for him. Evidence of her need glistened in the dim light, tempting him forward. He pushed off the bed and did away with his clothes then rejoined her, lying off to her side so he could explore every precious inch of her with his mouth and his hands. She tasted as good as she looked.

With deliberate slowness, he trailed a finger down over her collarbone then over to the inside of her arm, watching as she shivered. He then drew the digit across her chest then down to draw ever-smaller circles around her right nipple before touching the tip itself. If her thick swallow was anything to go by, she was enjoying the journey. And judging by his pulsing erection, he wasn't having such a bad time himself.

He switched his attention to her other nipple, watching as she arched her back the slightest bit as if tempting him to add his mouth to the mix. An offer no man could pass up. He ran his tongue the length of the distended flesh, then nibbled before taking it deep into his mouth. Her groan wound around him, tightening the muscles of his groin.

He sensed Reilly's growing desire to take control. To up the pace of their lovemaking. Which made him doubly glad when she didn't act on it. The trust of the action. The willingness to please him. Both made this more than just a simple sack session. What they were doing was more than sex. He could virtually feel the deepening of his feelings toward the gloriously naked woman lying next to him. He knew a need to bring her a pleasure no man before him had given her. He wanted to claim her in a way he had claimed no woman before her.

A few weeks ago the concept might have scared the hell out of him. He'd seen what happened to his friends when they'd fallen in love over the years. Saw them alter their lifestyle, change their ways, essentially transform into different people. But Reilly asked him to change nothing. She didn't comment on the color of his shirt, the meaning being that she wanted him to change into something else. She didn't look at his restaurant and tell him what was missing. She just…shared with him. No demands. No pressures. No obvious hint dropping. If anything, she seemed to be trying to maintain distance between them. Not because she wasn't interested. All he had to do was look into her face and know that she was as drawn to him as he was to her. No, she felt what was happening as profoundly as he did. And he suspected she might be scared. Of what, he couldn't be sure. But he could take a wild guess that his reputation with women wasn't helping any.

He drew his finger down the middle of her stomach, reveling in the silky smoothness of her skin. He dipped down lower until he was nearly touching the wedge of springy hair between her legs. She drew in a sharp breath and he watched as she opened her thighs even further to him.

Oh, he planned to get there all right. But in his own sweet time.

He knew she had to be going crazy right about

now. Yet she still allowed him to set the pace. Let him slide his fingers down the inside of her thigh then up over her pubic hair to the other thigh, purposely avoiding the place she most wanted him to touch. She moaned and arched her neck, her mouth split open, her eyes closed as she gave herself over to vivid sensation.

Ben slid over until he was between her legs then leaned over her, flicking his tongue over her stomach. She gasped and her hands automatically grabbed for him. He gently lay them back at her sides then flattened his fingers against her waist, holding her still as he retraced the path his fingers had taken with his mouth. Her skin was hot to the point of being feverish. Her stomach moved up and down with her quick, ragged breathing. He was aware that every time he dipped down for another taste, his chest teased her springy curls, pressed into her dampness. He spread her further to him, edging the glorious triangle with his tongue, breathing in her musky scent. He positioned his thumbs against the very outer fringe of hair and parted her, drawing out another moan. Then he softly blew on her exposed, swollen flesh.

She shuddered so violently with her climax the mattress quaked under them. Ben openly watched her, absorbing everything that was Reilly in the throes of orgasm. Then when the contractions began to ebb, he fastened his lips on the tiny bud in the middle of the nest of curls and drew the sensitive flesh deep into his mouth.

Reilly cried out, challenging the roar of the sea as her fists tangled in his sheets and her back came up off the bed, pressing herself harder against his mouth as she came again.

Ben kissed her along her inner thigh as her breathing slowed.

"Wow," she murmured, entangling her fingers in his hair.

Ben grinned against her skin then nipped her. She gave a little cry of surprise. "You ain't seen nothing yet."

And moments later, when he was sheathed with a condom and positioned against her dripping entrance, he was pretty sure he'd won her over to his side of the speed equation. Especially when he slowly entered her to the hilt and she immediately came again. And again. And again. Making him feel like he was an out-and-out sex god.

And making him fall even deeper for her with each passing minute....

REILLY AWOKE to the distant squeal of sea lions and seagulls, feeling more relaxed and rested than she could ever remember feeling in her life. She cracked her eyelids open, watching the play of light on water against the ceiling.

Then she jackknifed upright in Ben's empty, king-size desperately searching for a clock. She finally found one by means of an alarm clock that had been stuck inside a drawer next to the bed.

Ten minutes after nine.

She gave a squeal of her own and leaped from the bed, scrambling for her discarded dress and shoes. The underwear she could do without. She should have opened the doors to Sugar 'n' Spice over three hours ago. She should have started baking the day's take even before that.

She looked around for any sign of Ben and found none. A square of white on the other pillow caught her eye. She snatched up the note and read it:

I didn't have the heart to wake you so I found Tina's number in your purse and asked her to open the shop for you. I'm at the restaurant. Stop by for a cuppa on your way out.

The note was signed simply, *B.*

He'd gone through her purse? He'd called Tina? Stop by for a cuppa?

Reilly fought the urge to crawl back under the covers and stay there until the repercussions of Ben's actions blew over.

Which would probably be never.

She found the purse in question on the opposite bedside table and snatched it up. She opened it, trying to look at it through Ben's eyes. Vitamins, appetite suppressors, lip gloss, a brush and her address book. Nothing overly personal. Nothing she should be upset at him seeing.

The problem was she was very upset.

And if she stopped by Benardo's Hideaway on her

way home it wouldn't be for a cuppa, it would be to dump the cup's contents over his unthinking head.

Oh, God. She rushed for the door, stopping briefly before opening it to gather her wits about her. What kind of damage control could she possibly wield to cover up this one? Tina was probably at the shop just waiting to bombard her with dozens of questions the moment she walked through the door. And Lord forbid Layla, Mallory or Jack happened to stop by this morning for a sticky bun.

And what about everyone at the restaurant? If she showed up in the same dress she'd been wearing the night before, wouldn't they know something was up?

Of course, they would, stupid.

As she climbed into the shop van, she could only be glad that she'd insisted on driving out to the restaurant the night before instead of having Ben pick her up. At least she'd be able to get home on her own without having to call for a taxi, or worse, call one of her friends to pick her up.

As for Ben…

Of all the arrogant, self-serving, invasively…sweet things for him to do.

As she drove down the road leading back to the restaurant and the highway beyond, she felt a smile creep across her face. How long had it been since she'd slept in? As for the waking to the sound of the ocean part, the answer to that was easy: never. More than six months had passed since she hadn't gotten up at four-thirty to start baking. And even on Sundays, when she opened the shop later, she was wide awake by five no matter how late she'd stayed up the night before, her body clock refusing to respond to her attempts to smack its snooze button.

The minivan bearing the shop's name bounced over the dirt road as she drew closer and closer to the restaurant. She noticed an electrician's van out back. And spotted Ben consulting with Lance at the back door of the restaurant. Her heart gave a thick triple beat as he cupped his hand over his eyes, watching her approach. But as her front tires hit paved road, she accelerated, giving him no more than a brief wave as she sped by.

She'd have to deal with him later. Right now she had bigger fish to fry. *Much* bigger fish.

10

THE DAY ONLY GREW progressively worse from there. Forget the nonstop questions that Tina pelted at Reilly the instant she arrived to take over for her teenaged pain-in-the-butt niece. Reilly didn't have nearly enough ready stock on hand to take care of customer needs. Even Efi had called from the pay phone at school to see what all the fuss was about because Ben had called Tina at home and Tina had generously shared that a man had called on Reilly's behalf, which undoubtedly meant that Reilly had slept at the man-in-question's house and that this had to be serious. At least that was her sister Debbie's rationale when she called three times, unhappy with the answers she was getting.

No, she wasn't bringing him to Thanksgiving dinner at the folks next week. No, they weren't going to meet him anytime soon, if at all. No, there was no engagement ring on the horizon. No, Tina couldn't be the maid of honor because there wasn't going to be a wedding. And, ultimately, no, she couldn't possibly cater her own reception because, well, there wasn't going to be one of those, either.

To top it off, it seemed foot traffic was heavier than

usual. And considering the display case was emptier than usual, she wasn't making a good impression on potential regulars. And if it wasn't one of her sisters or her nieces on the phone, it was a potential client having read about her in the *Confidential* and wanting price quotes. She liked the last caller best. She'd wanted to know if she could make one hundred penis-shaped cakes with fleshlike frosting for a bachelorette party later on in the month.

She'd almost given in to that one, if only to see if she could do it. But ultimately she decided she didn't want to be known for penis cakes. She couldn't see herself twenty years from now making penis cakes for bachelorette parties.

And where would she be twenty years from now?

Funny, where once she saw herself with a half dozen shops, having dinner with her friends and living a happy and fancy-free life, now all she drew was a big, fat blank. Well, when Ben's face didn't pop up to fill the void, that is.

She took a mixed batch of sticky buns and cream horns minus the cream out of the oven, wiped her hands on her apron and made her way back to the front of the shop.

She hesitated as she took in where Mallory sat at her friends' usual corner table stirring five pounds of sugar into her ounce of coffee. As she settled back into the seat across from her friend, she supposed the one thing she could be thankful for was that Layla,

Mallory and Jack were still in the dark about this morning's fiasco.

Mallory finished with her coffee then began forking around the edges of a frozen solid slice of chocolate cheesecake that Reilly had ferreted out of the freezer for her for lunch.

Tina had—thankfully!—left for class about a half hour ago. Johnnie Thunder was hooked up to his laptop across the shop. And another customer, a middle-aged male, was sitting at another table reading the paper while drinking an extra large cup of regular coffee, two sugars.

"Oh! I almost forgot why I stopped by," Mallory said. Before Reilly went to check the oven, her friend had been talking about her lack of luck finding a decent shoot sight for her latest documentary.

Reilly hiked a brow and fidgeted. She had to be the worst liar in the entire world. Not that keeping last night's activities from Mallory was a lie, exactly. But it wasn't telling the truth, either. "I thought you came by to raid the display case, as usual."

Mallory made a face. "How little you know." She glanced toward the pitifully empty area in question. "Anyway, I'd be sadly disappointed if I had come for that reason. What happened? Did a busful of tourists clean you out this morning or something?"

Reilly scratched her head, wishing she'd had a chance to take a shower before coming down to the shop. She'd combed through most of the products she'd used on her hair the night before, but it was all making her itch something terrible.

Aside from the fact that she was afraid that Mallory would be able to smell sex from sixty paces. "Something like that."

"Anyway," Mall said, sticking her fork into the frozen center of her cake then taking a paper out of her ever present backpack. "I picked this up on the Metro this morning. The things people leave on the seats."

"Mmm," Reilly absently agreed, never having ridden L.A.'s subway system. But since Mallory's battle-scarred twenty-year-old car had finally bitten the dust recently, she'd had to resort to alternate modes of transportation. That was when she couldn't con Jack into shuttling her around.

She realized she was staring at Mallory's T-shirt, which this morning read, Men is a Four-Letter Word, and shook her head.

The shop's telephone rang as Mallory looked through the secondhand paper.

"Excuse me," Reilly said, almost relieved for the interruption and trying not to run away from the table. She was this close to blurting something along the lines of "I spent the night at Ben's last night and we had the most incredible sex I've ever had in my life and then I woke up to find out that not only had he gone through my purse but that he'd called my sister's house and life has been a mess ever since." Just like that. Without taking a breath.

She felt Mallory's curious gaze on her back and wondered if she'd just given up the ghost with the turbo speed she ran from the table. She wouldn't be surprised if her friend could have intuited what she'd just been thinking.

"Sugar 'n' Spice," she said into the telephone receiver.

"And I can personally vouch that the owner tastes like both." Ben's sexy voice filled her ear.

Reilly immediately turned away from the sitting area, heat surging to all points south. God but the things he did to her.

She realized she was about to make a humongous mistake by taking the phone into the kitchen with her and said, "Yes, we cater."

"Excuse me?" Ben said with a chuckle.

Reilly forced herself to face back toward the tables then took her notepad out of her apron pocket. "For a hundred? Certainly. Why don't we schedule a time for us to go over what you're looking for?"

Silence.

Reilly smiled at where Mallory was watching her oddly and where Johnnie Thunder's fingers had frozen over his keyboard.

She said, "Six o'clock tonight? I happen to have that time open."

Ben cleared his throat. "Does that mean you want me to come over at six?"

"Yes, yes. Very well then. We'll see you tonight."

Reilly hung up the phone, pretended to scribble

something onto her notepad when she was really using the time to calm her heart and regain control over her erratic breathing. It was natural for a woman to have that sustained, heart-pounding reaction to a man, wasn't it? Surely at some point she would just smile at the thought of him instead of getting so hot even a cold shower wouldn't be able to cool her.

Okay, this wasn't helping. She slipped the pad and pen back into her pocket.

"New customer?" Mallory asked when she sat back down.

Reilly felt every inch of exposed skin grow hot all over again. "Yes. A recommendation from Layla's stepmother if you can believe it."

"Mmm. Anyway, this is what I wanted to show you."

Reilly distractedly looked down at the folded paper Mallory had pushed in front of her. Her eyes widened.

She hadn't known what she'd expected. A review of one of Mallory's recent documentaries, perhaps? Or even a copy of one of Jack's columns that had pissed her friend off—Jack's male-oriented point of view tended to do that a lot.

What she got instead was a picture of Ben Kane with a drop-dead gorgeous redhead hanging from his arm. Danish model Heidi Klutzenhoffer was how the caption identified her.

Reilly suddenly felt sick.

"It was taken at a wrap party last weekend," Mallory said, pointing out the date and the details.

Last weekend... Saturday... One of the nights Ben had said he didn't have plans he couldn't cancel.... The night she and Efi had gorged on Italian, watched DVDs and moaned about Greek school.

She slowly shook her head, connecting the dots. Friday Ben came by at midnight to feed her dinner and get a gander at her granny panties. Saturday she'd spent with Efi. Then Monday night he'd come by her apartment and she'd essentially mauled him on the sofa.

Between Friday night and Monday night loomed a huge gap that it seemed Ms. Heidi Klutzenhoffer had been all too happy to fill.

She leaned her head against her hand, feeling the hotness of her skin. "So?" she said, trying to play off the event. After all, nothing had really happened between them Friday night. They kissed, petted a little, then she'd pushed him through the door.

Still, it didn't stop her from feeling...used, somehow.

Mallory made a face. "So maybe I was wrong. Maybe your going out with Mr. Hot Pants isn't the greatest idea in the world, Rei."

Too late, she silently offered up.

"You're too good for the dog, is all I'm saying. And I'm afraid that if you got involved with him, it would lead to nothing but heartbreak."

Doubly too late, Reilly thought.

She offered up a vague smile. "Who said I was even considering getting involved with him?"

Mallory stuffed the paper back into her backpack. "God, Reilly, what are we in high school? I know that's who you were talking to a minute ago. I also know you weren't home last night when I called at eleven o'clock." Reilly opened her mouth. "And that you weren't down here, either, because I tried."

Reilly snapped her mouth back shut.

There m   have been something on Reilly's face that she ha   meant for her friend to see because Mallory's expression instantly changed. God, how she hated pity. "Oh, sweetie," Mall said, reaching for her hands. It was all Reilly could do not to slap them away. "I just don't want to see you get hurt, that's all. Neither do Layla and Jack."

Reilly widened her eyes. "They know?"

"Of course they know. I conferenced with them this morning after I saw the piece. And they're as concerned as I am."

Great. Was there a single person on earth who didn't know she had a mad crush on the high school football captain?

Worse, that she had shoved him into the proverbial back seat at the drive-in? Twice?

Reilly patted Mallory's hands back then smiled. "I appreciate your concern, Mall. The last thing I intend to do is get hurt by the likes of Ben Kane." She shrugged and crossed her arms over her chest. She recognized the defensive action and forced herself to drop her hands to her sides. "I'm no dummy. I knew...know what I'm getting myself into."

Mallory rolled her eyes. "If you give me that whole 'it's better to have loved and lost than never to have loved at all' mumbo jumbo, I'm going to bean you with my frozen cheesecake."

"That's not what I was going to say." She cleared her throat. "What I was going to say is that I'm a consenting adult. He's a consenting adult. And whatever happens beyond that is between us."

"Whoa. This is high school."

Reilly wanted to scream. "No, Mall. This would be high school if I told you I wasn't seeing him and went ahead and did so anyway."

"Good point." She returned to her cheesecake. "Just don't say I didn't tell you so, you know, when things take a nosedive."

"Jesus! Why are you so damn pessimistic all the time? Is it a skill you were born with, or is it something you developed along the way?"

Mallory blinked at her.

Okay, so she never lost her temper. But certainly even she deserved to get pissy every now and again. Years before, food had provided an outlet. In more recent years, running and the shop. Now, there wasn't anything that could prevent her outburst. How was she supposed to respond to what Mallory was saying?

Damn it, she liked the guy.

Too much.

Mallory regained her composure before Reilly did. "Let's just say that I've had my heart trampled by Ben Kane's type more times than I care to admit."

Reilly ground her back teeth. "And you're convinced that I'm going to end up just like you."

"No, I'm trying to stop you from ending up just like me." Mallory sat back and sighed heavily. "Look, if you doubt what I'm saying, ask him about Holly—"

"Heidi," Reilly corrected.

"Whatever. Ask him about Miss Silicone Danish World and see what he says. If he comes back with some 'all in the line of business, babe' answer, then, well, you'll have yours."

"And how's that?"

Her friend looked at her watch. "Because then you'll know that that's not the last time you'll hear that excuse." She scooted from her chair. "Look, I've got to go. Do you have a container for this or something? Maybe it will thaw out on the subway."

"Just make sure you keep it a long way away from your frozen heart," Reilly muttered as she slid off her own chair and went to get her a container.

Mallory caught Reilly's hand after she'd put the cake in a bag then handed it to her friend. "You know, I'm not trying to be a killjoy or anything, Rei. It's just…it's just I know guys. And Ben Kane? He's got nothing but heartache written all over him."

Reilly felt her eyes burn. Maybe her friend was right. Because what she was feeling right now could be in no way connected to happy. "Thanks, Mall."

"Don't mention it, kid."

As she watched her friend leave the shop, however,

she had to wonder how much of the growing pain she was feeling was due solely to her well-meaning friend, and how much to Ben.

Then again, you couldn't create pain where there wasn't already fertile ground for it to grow.

She turned on her heel toward the kitchen. For God's sake, why did Ben Kane choose her damn door to walk through?

She pushed the swinging door open then nearly tripped over the cat that had adopted her. "Geez, Louise! Watch it, Cat."

After making sure she had her balance, she picked up the ragged black feline. She had been calling it simply "Cat" since she'd found it on her doorstep last week, but he wasn't responding well to it.

"How about Louise, huh?" She turned him around. Yep, definitely a male. When she turned him back around to face her, she found his eyes narrowed like he was saying, "Having fun back there?" "Louise doesn't have to be a feminine name. It could be the Mexican version of Louis. Or, more accurately, Luis. How does that sound?"

He meowed caustically at her.

"Fine? How about Satan then?"

She made a face at him then put him back down. He followed her toward the back of the shop where she opened the door and put some dry food out for him in the alley. Efi had bought him a bowl with cat paws all over it.

As Reilly leaned against the open doorjamb and

watched him eat, she wondered why she had never considered that the cat was black before. What did they say about black cats crossing your path?

She headed back inside and slammed the door. What did they say about single women with cats who couldn't seem to get their shit together?

She scrubbed her hands then set about immersing herself in her work. At least that was one area of her life that never let her down.

11

"THE LINE WAS CUT at the pole," the electrician told Ben and Lance a little while later. "Clean cut, too. No mistaking this was done purposely."

Ben rubbed the back of his neck. That didn't make any sense. Who would want to cause him trouble?

"I ain't gonna be able to fix it, either," the electrician went on. "Edison's gonna have to send someone out. That's their territory. I mess with them, I get my license revoked."

Ben thanked the man then left him to work out whatever business remained with Lance. He pushed open the door to his office then sank into his plush leather chair. Lord only knew when Edison would have someone out there. Given the remoteness of the restaurant, and the fact that the outage didn't affect other nearby residents, he probably ranked pretty low on the priority list.

Then again, if anyone could figure something out, Lance could. He leaned forward and looked at the invoices on his desk. Invoices for the wrong orders. He flipped on his computer then entered the online ordering system. You needed to have the correct username and password in order to access their account.

And only Ben, Lance and the accountant had access. Lance had gone through and changed both passwords the day before and his accountant had recommended they change them daily until they could clear up the problem.

He stared down at the log that outlined the change of orders. All appeared to be made from the restaurant computer. And all during the time either he or Lance or both of them had been there.

It didn't make any sense.

He eyed the telephone receiver.

Of course, Reilly's strange behavior when he called a little while ago didn't make much sense, either.

He put his hand out and touched the receiver, then tapped on it and pulled his hand back. He couldn't call her again. He'd look…desperate.

He grinned. Well, that was only fitting because he was increasingly becoming more desperate—namely to spend more time with Reilly.

When he'd awakened that morning to find her sweet body curved against his, he'd had an epiphany of sorts. Rather than the immediate panic that usually filled him when he woke up to find he'd spent the night with a woman, he'd felt…at peace. Whole somehow. And so damn happy that it had taken an hour to wipe the grin from his face.

Something like that had never happened to him before.

While the thought should have scared him, it

didn't. Instead, it made him even goofier still. Finally he was finding out what it meant to love somebody.

Not just somebody but Reilly Chudowski.

He now understood what his father had felt when he met his mother and married her three weeks later at an Elvis ceremony in Las Vegas.

How every last one of his friends had felt when they'd given up bachelorhood for the chance to wake up next to that one woman every morning.

How it felt to know that you'd found that one person in the entire world who simply got you.

The telephone rang. He sat up in his chair, hoping it would be Reilly. He picked it up on the second ring without looking at the caller ID display.

"Ben, baby, where have you been? I've been trying to get a hold of you forever."

Heidi Klutzenhoffer.

Where hearing from the leggy redhead would have made him happy just the week before, now it only made him feel...uncomfortable somehow. Now that he knew the difference between what he could feel for a woman, and what he had felt before, it didn't matter that Heidi was every man's wet dream. The only person who could do that for him anymore was Reilly.

"Hello, Heidi. I'm sorry you've had so much trouble getting through. There's been a lot going on here lately."

"And here I thought you were trying to avoid me," she purred in a voice that had landed her some commercial voice-overs and had just gotten her a role in an upcoming Colin Farrell movie involving vampires. The sexy redhead would be the perfect foil for the latest Hollywood bad boy, especially if she were cast as one of the bloodsucking vampires.

Last Saturday had marked their third outing together. A match made in PR heaven. Literally. His publicist had met up with her publicist and all had been in agreement that since both of them were currently in between steadies it would help them to be seen together. So he'd taken her first to a charity event, then to a golf outing and finally to the feature film wrap party last Saturday night. Sure enough, on all three occasions they'd landed a photo in nearly every paper in L.A. and he even understood one of the national rags had picked up a shot or two. Of course the headline in the national rag nearly made him choke—something about the two of them adopting pets from the city pound to satisfy certain…sexual appetites—but as his publicist told him, only no publicity was bad publicity.

He absently scratched his chin. What was it that made his reaction to Heidi so different from his feelings for Reilly? Okay, so it didn't help that on all three of their outings Heidi obsessed about the way she looked every other second, and demanded his attention on the offbeat seconds. She had a dry sense of humor and he suspected she was more intelligent than your average model. He had even enjoyed her company. On strictly a friendship level. He hadn't slept with her on the first two occasions because he'd needed to get back to the restaurant—or had that been an excuse? And last Saturday...well, all night his mind had been on another woman he had just met and who had captivated him.

Who continued to captivate him.

He rubbed his brow line, wondering what Heidi wanted. "How could you ever think I would want to avoid a wildcat like you?"

She appeared to like the comparison and laughed throatily. "Well, then, I take it you'd be up for taking me to the Affleck-Damon premiere next weekend, then?"

The word "no" sat on the tip of his tongue. And remained there. It wouldn't be proper etiquette to turn her down flat immediately after her proposal. He glanced at his calendar and noticed that the following weekend was Thanksgiving.

Of course. The beginning of the Christmas movie season. And seeing as the latest Ben Affleck and Matt Damon collaboration had the biggest box office buzz this year, the premiere would be well covered....

Reilly...a voice whispered in his head.

"As luck would have it, I have something on my calendar for that night, Heidi," he said.

"Oh, no!"

He dry washed his face, hating the sound of disappointment in her voice. It wasn't her fault that she just didn't do it for him. Maybe he should let her down a little more gently. "But let me call my publicist and see if there's some way I can get out of it."

"That sounds more like my Benny," she purred.

Ben cringed. His only intention was to call his publicist and have him make his apologies to Heidi first thing tomorrow morning. There was no way in hell he was going to that premiere with her. Not when he could be spending the time with Reilly instead.

After talking about mundane things like the warm weather and the latest Hollywood gossip, he ended the call and was just about to put another in to his publicist when Lance appeared in the doorway. "You're not going to believe this order...."

MALLORY'S WORDS of warning against Ben haunted Reilly throughout the rest of the day. Of course it didn't help that Layla had called at around three to repeat, albeit in a more civilized way, what Mall had said. Reilly was absently surprised that Jack hadn't said anything when she'd called him and asked if he was available to make some deliveries for her in the morning because Tina had an early class. Then again, Jack wouldn't say anything. Rather his words would be stamped all over his handsome face.

She should have hired the pimply kid she'd interviewed that afternoon for the delivery position who'd only had his license for a week. Anything would be better than having to see Jack's frown of disapproval.

But, more than anything, the fact that it was half-past six and Ben was late lent a credence to Mallory's words that Reilly was loathe to admit, but recognized just the same.

She was upstairs in her apartment, having showered and changed then worked herself into another sweat with all her pacing. Usually the movement helped her think. But not now.

She eyed the clock. She had said six, hadn't she? Yes, she had. While everything else about the day emerged a chaotic blur, that part she remembered clear as a bell.

She'd asked him to come over at six.

And it was now six-thirty.

Damn.

She grabbed her apartment keys then slid into her flip-flops. If she was going to be restless, she might as well be restless downstairs where she could put it to good use. She had an order for tomorrow afternoon that she could get a head start on. Then there was the mess she'd left because she had finished up later than she had anticipated. What did Ben think? That she didn't have anything better to do than sit around and wait for him? She was a busy woman. A busy businesswoman with lots to fill her time with. She wasn't about to sit around waiting for whenever he could spare her a minute.

She reached for the door handle at the same time someone knocked on the door.

She jumped back to stare at it. Okay, that was creepy.

In fact, there were more than a few things that gave her the creeps lately.

A quick clearing of her throat and then, ''Come in.''

Her visitor—she hoped it was Ben—tried the handle with no luck. Reilly had forgotten she had locked it.

She stuck her thumbnail between her teeth. Was it a sign, maybe? That perhaps she should leave Ben on the other side of the door and tell him she couldn't see him again?

She rolled her eyes as she stared at where Luis was winding around her ankles. What was it with her and signs lately? She wasn't superstitious. She wasn't even particularly religious.

She unlocked the door then allowed him to open it. *I'm not a doormat, I'm not a doormat,* she repeated to herself.

But the moment she saw him she felt like lying down in front of him and inviting him to wipe his feet on her. That was her physical reaction. Then she noticed his drawn look, his five o'clock shadow, and just felt concern.

''You look awful,'' she said.

He gave her a half smile. ''Yeah, well, I feel pretty awful, so why shouldn't I look it?''

A small voice in her head demanded to know why he was late, why he hadn't had the courtesy to call and who in the hell that Heidi woman was anyway. But it wasn't her voice. It was Mallory's.

Her voice? It made her invite him to sit down, made her go into the kitchen for an ice-cold beer, then sit down next to him.

"Sorry, I'm late," he said after he'd taken a healthy sip. "I would have called, but by the time I realized I was so late I was almost here."

"You don't have to explain," she said, cringing the instant the words were out of her mouth.

He offered up a genuine closed mouth smile. "Yes, I do."

"Okay, yes, you do."

"It's just…"

She waited for him to continue, resisting the urge to gesture with her hand in a prompting manner. Like a wheel regaining momentum.

Then it struck her. The reason he was late. The reason behind his not looking at her the way he usually did.

Oh, God. He was going to dump her.

"It's just…" he said again.

"It's Heidi, isn't it?" Reilly took his beer and downed half of it. She realized he was watching her and she smiled foolishly then wiped the back of her hand across her mouth.

She had *not* just done that!

"Heidi? Oh, you must mean Heidi Klutzenhoffer. No, this isn't about her. Heidi was nothing but an occasional appearance companion. Nothing more."

"Was? As in past tense?"

"Was." He chuckled quietly. "Looks like you had the kind of day I did."

"Depends on what kind of day you had," she said carefully.

Well, chalk one up for Mallory. She would get a chance to tell her "I told you so" sooner than even Reilly had believed. Ben was about to dump her. Then again, could she really blame him? Here he was one of the most eligible bachelors in L.A. and this morning she had raced from his place like a bat out of hell with barely a wave after having had one of the most incredible nights of her life. Then to top all that off she'd pretended he was a client when he called later because Mallory had been in the shop and she hadn't wanted her friend to know she was talking to him, even though Mall had figured it out anyway.

And now she was an out-and-out doormat just waiting to be replaced by a newer model.

"This was one of the most difficult days of my life," Ben said.

Reilly's throat closed and she had to force herself not to reach for his beer again and drain the rest of it.

"For the first time in seven years I had to close the doors to Benardo's Hideaway due to circumstances beyond my control."

Reilly blinked once. Twice. Her heart beat an unsteady rhythm in her chest.

He wasn't telling her to get lost.

He was sharing a difficult moment with her.

"Is that all?" she blurted.

Ben blinked at her.

Reilly smacked her forehead with the heel of her hand. "I'm sorry. You're right. It has been a difficult day for me, too. Although not as difficult as your day, apparently." She rested her hand on his shoulder, feeling his taut muscles beneath. She began to knead them. "What happened?" she asked.

He grinned at her. Not a half-assed attempt, but a full-out Ben Kane knee-wobbler. Reilly caught her breath. "You first."

She shook her head. "No. I didn't have to close shop. You had to close your restaurant." She worked her fingers along the ridge of his neck. "Is it because of the electricity?"

"No. Yes." He sighed and sank down farther into the cushions. "The power's still out, but that's not the reason I closed the doors." She watched as he closed his eyes. Was it her, or was he relaxing under the simple power of her touch.

Oh, she liked this.

She scooted a little closer so she could better work the muscles of his left shoulder.

"Fabio, the head chef, called in. It seems he was mugged in the parking lot of the meat market we work with."

"Oh, God! Nothing serious, I hope?"

He cracked his eyelids open. "Mmm. That feels good. Continue doing what you're doing...."

She did, feeling a strange kind of joy at her being able to ease his tension in such a small way.

"Is Fabio okay?" she asked.

"No. I mean, yes. His injury wasn't life-threatening."

"Injury?"

He nodded and his eyes closed again, allowing her to concentrate on the sexy line of his mouth. "The mugger slammed his left hand in his car door. Ten bones cracked right in two."

Reilly gasped.

She'd noticed the night before that Fabio was a lefty. That meant—

"Yeah, that means he's pretty much out of the kitchen until he heals."

"Oh, Ben, I'm so sorry. Fabio must be devastated."

"That's the word I was looking for," he said, sinking even further into the sofa. "I could see he was devastated when I picked Fabio up from the hospital then called Lance to let him know what was happening." His frown lines deepened. "I could have sworn the guy was a kind word away from blubbering."

"Cooking is his life."

Ben nodded. "Yeah."

Reilly tried to move to his other shoulder but couldn't reach so she began to straddle him. He squinted up at her, his mouth turning up into a suggestive grin. "Now that's a move designed to make any man forget his troubles."

She lightly whacked him. "This isn't about sex, you maniac." She felt his instant hard-on between her thighs and wondered if she could take the words back. "It's about making you feel better."

"That would make me feel better."

She watched where he was skimming his hand down her waist toward her crotch. She caught his arm and laid it back down by his side. "Would you just relax? I took a massage therapy course one year. I know what I'm doing."

He closed his eyes. "I'll say." He scooted down further so that his erection rested more solidly between her legs. "And what move would this be?"

"That move would be the 'if you don't stop wriggling I'm going to do some major damage' move."

"Ah. Sounds painful."

"You have no idea."

She smiled as she said the words because, despite his suggestive behavior, Ben was relaxing. Well, all but one part of him. She noticed his muscles slacken under her careful ministrations. Watched the tense planes of his face soften.

He quietly cleared his throat. "So tonight we go your way?" he asked.

She twisted her lips, working on a particularly stubborn knot in his right shoulder. "How do you mean?"

"Fast...or slow."

Sex. He was talking about sex again.

And her body was responding in a way that said it was more than open to the idea.

But her mind…

"You know," she said quietly. "You better watch out or I'll start to suspect that you want me just for the easy sex."

The pleasure disappeared from his face and he opened his eyes fully to take her in. "Trust me, Reilly, if this—whatever this is that is happening between us—was just about the sex, I wouldn't be here right now."

For some stupid reason, his response delighted her in a way she couldn't even begin to analyze right now. Of course, he could also mean that sex with her wasn't good enough to be just about the sex, but she chose to ignore that. For now anyway. She was sure she'd probably fret about that part of it at two in the morning when she should be sleeping.

She leaned forward and kissed him. "I like that," she said softly.

He waggled his brows at her. "How much?"

She laughed then ordered him to close his eyes again.

For a long time, neither of them said anything as she slid her hands and fingers up and over his arms and shoulders then up to his temples. She was half-afraid he'd fallen asleep, until he hummed in approval when she worked on his hands, finger by finger.

"You know," she said quietly. "All doesn't have to be lost. You know, in terms of the restaurant."

His gaze was questioning.

She shrugged. "I was just thinking…Fabio's injury

isn't completely debilitating. Meaning he could still physically be present at the restaurant, right?''

Ben nodded. ''Right,'' he said hesitantly.

''Well, then, he could just supervise the other cooks. You know, teach them how to make the dishes the way he would. No, he might not be able to chop veggies or dice the meat, but I don't see why he couldn't do everything else.''

She watched as a grin slowly began to spread across his face. Then she stilled when he slid his hands up over her arms across her jaw then threaded his fingers into her hair so he could draw her down for a kiss. ''You're a genius.''

Right now she'd settle for bed bunny.

He gave her another kiss, this one long and leisurely. She felt a different kind of tension build up in him and transfer to her, making her all hot and wet. God, but he felt good. Too good. And while the sensation should have scared her, for some reason it didn't. Instead she found herself merely enjoying the ride, ready to take this…thing between them as far as it would go.

She pulled back slightly from him and rested her forehead against his. She waggled her eyebrows at him. ''Now, about this sex thing…'' she said in her best seductive voice.

12

"MOM SAYS you're acting like a whore."

The following Monday morning, Reilly nearly spewed coffee all over the top of the table she and fifteen-going-on-forty-year-old Efi were sitting at in the front corner of Sugar 'n' Spice. Five days had passed since Ben had called her sister's house making excuses for her so she could sleep in. Five bliss-filled days of Ben coming by her place every night. Of exploring each other's bodies. Of exploring each other's lives.

And now she was being made to pay for it.

"I think the word you're looking for is slut," Reilly said, wiping her mouth and hoping coffee wasn't dripping from her nose. "A whore gets paid. A slut just does it for the pleasure. Your mom was never really good at telling the difference."

Efi smiled, her pink hair looking particularly bright with the morning sunlight on it. "You know, that's what I thought. But I wouldn't dare use either word in front of Mom or else she'd ground me for life."

"Sounds like my sister. I'm surprised she used the word in front of you."

Efi toyed with a sticky bun she wasn't really eating.

"She didn't. She was talking to grandma on the phone and I was eavesdropping."

Oh, boy. The one person she hadn't heard from yet was her mother regarding Ben's curious activities last week. She had a feeling that was going to change fairly quickly.

"So," Reilly said, not about to go further down that path with her niece. "Why did you get up an hour earlier than you have to to come by here before school?"

Efi shrugged with one shoulder as if it was no big deal. Only they both knew what a big deal it was because Efi slept like the dead. "I came by to see if I could help out."

Reilly glanced to where Tina was helping a customer. "What, for a whole fifteen minutes?" She stared at Efi through her lashes. "Don't tell me. This is about Jason again."

Efi turned about ten shades of red but shook her head. "No. Actually there's a new guy...."

And her sister was calling *her* a slut?

She blinked, wondering if she'd really just thought that about her own niece. "At high school?"

Efi shook her head. "No, at Greek school. His family just moved from Astoria or somewhere."

"That's in New York City."

Efi nodded again. "Anyway, his name is Kostas and, well..."

"You like him."

Efi nodded. "He's only a year older than me and

he seems nice and everything, and every time I look at him, he's looking at me, but...he hasn't talked to me yet.''

Well at least she wasn't saying she hated Greek school anymore. Her sister Debbie must be celebrating.

She asked, ''And have you talked to him?''

''No.'' Efi rolled her eyes then stared at her as if she'd gone soft in the head. ''Mom says girls don't talk to guys first. They wait for the guys to approach them.''

Her sister, the hypocrite. Reilly guessed Debbie hadn't shared the story about how she'd met her husband, Efi's father, at a Greek festival and made out with him the first night behind the gyro stand after everyone had gone home for the night.

The cowbell above the door jingled. Reilly didn't see who had entered but knew immediately by the smell of his woodsy aftershave. ''Hi, Jack.''

She heard him sigh before he walked into her line of sight. ''It's my cologne, isn't it? The reason I can never sneak up on any of you.''

Reilly smiled at him. ''That and our hunk radar alert. It goes off when you're around.''

''Ha, ha.'' He looked to Efi. ''Hey, squirt,'' he said, ruffling the top of her pink head. ''Like the hair color.''

If Reilly had ruffled her niece's carefully gelled hair there would have been hell to pay. But Efi not only let Jack do it, she was all smiles and pink cheeks. "Thanks, Jack."

He looked back at Reilly. "Are the deliveries ready to go?"

She nodded. "Yeah. Only a couple of trays from the refrigerator to put in the van and you're all set." She smiled at him. "Thanks for doing this, Jack."

"What are friends for?"

Thinking back on her conversations with Mallory and Layla, she wondered what friends were for, indeed.

Along with every other female in the place, she watched Jack walk toward the kitchen. She heard his mumbled curses indicating he knew they were all looking. Of course, Reilly didn't think what she was doing fell into friendship territory, but, hey, she was only human.

And so was Efi, if her rapt attention on Jack's tight, yummy behind was any indication.

"He's all that and a double cherry coke," Efi said with a sigh.

"I'm not even going to ask what that means." Reilly made a face. "Anyway, as I was saying before we were so welcomely interrupted, if we women waited for the guys to approach us, we'd never date." Even as she said the words, she wondered about her own dating methods up until that point. Ben had practically had to seduce a "yes" right out of her.

Efi's mouth gaped open. "That's what I told Mom."

"So, then, what's the real reason you haven't talked to him yet?"

Efi seemed to be paying too close attention to her sticky bun. "I don't know." She gave another of those one-shoulder shrugs. "I guess I'm afraid he'll think I'm stupid or something. You know, a hick."

Reilly laughed then abruptly stopped when Efi glared at her. "You're from L.A., Efi, not Toledo."

"Where's Toledo?"

"It's a city in Ohio. But that's not my point. My point is that I highly doubt he's going to think you're stupid for talking to him." She dared another sip of coffee. "Ask where he's from. What high school he's going to. What he thinks of Southern California. That kind of thing."

"But I already know the answers to those questions."

Reilly stared at her. "Then ask him out for a hot dog."

"A hot dog?"

"Okay, a piece of baklava. Bring him here. Tell him you need a New Yorker's opinion on western baklava."

"That's so lame."

"Yes, it is, isn't it? But lame is a step up from stupid." Reilly glanced at the clock on the wall. "Anyway, eat up or you're going to be late for school."

Efi pushed the sticky bun away. "I'm going to be

late anyway, so why don't you just call in sick for me and I'll hang out here and help out?''

So now she hated high school. Complicated role, playing aunt to a fifteen-year-old girl.

Reilly shook her head. "Not if helping out is what you just did here." She smiled. "Anyway, I value my life. Your mother would skin me alive if I contributed to your delinquency."

"You'd be teaching me a career."

Reilly got a bag from behind the counter and put the uneaten sticky bun into it. "What good would that do if you're illiterate?"

Efi rolled her eyes as she slid off her stool. "I learned how to read in the first grade, Aunt Rei."

"Yeah, but not the really big words. Like capital punishment. Which is what your mom will be facing after she kills me." She handed Efi the bag then gave her a gentle push toward the door. "Go."

Efi kissed her on the cheek and went. Reilly stood at the window watching her. Interesting how when the girl got ten paces away her step picked up, almost as if she'd already forgotten what they talked about.

Ah, to be fifteen again.

Then again, no.

She turned away from the window and cleaned off the table, passing by Johnnie Thunder where he sat in his usual spot again this morning. "Can I get you a refill?" she asked him.

He seemed surprised to find her standing next to him and pushed a button that made his laptop computer screen go blank. "Um, no. Thanks," he said almost sheepishly.

"No, problem," Reilly said, stopping to ask the other two customers if they were good to go before she headed behind the counter.

Tina's heavy sigh reached Reilly from the counter. "I don't know how you stand it, Aunt Rei," she said. "Efi's neurotic episodes. Mom and I don't have the patience." She sighed again as she slid a tray of scones back into the case. "God, I don't remember ever being that young."

Funny, Reilly thought, the last time she looked Tina was still that young.

"Anyway, Jack's waiting back in the kitchen," Tina said. "Do you want me to handle him?"

Her older niece's dark eyes were a little too bright, her smile a little too...predatory. "I think what you meant to say is should you handle the situation." She shook her head, took two sticky buns and put them into a bag, filled an extra large coffee cup, then went back for another sticky bun before closing the bag. "And, no, thank you. I'll...handle him myself."

She ignored Tina's horrified gasp and could only imagine what was going through her mind following "The Ben Incident." At this point, her family probably thought she was sleeping with every single male in the greater Los Angeles area. Then again, why stop with males? It was L.A., after all.

She pushed into the kitchen and found Jack sitting

reading the morning paper at the extra large island designed to handle the biggest orders.

"Ah, a woman after my own heart," he said, accepting the coffee then looking inside the bag. "Three? I must have been a very good boy indeed."

Reilly laughed as she took the chair next to him. "You have been."

He devoured half a roll then took a long sip of coffee. "Care to fill me in on what I did? You know, in case I decide I like the treatment?"

"Aside from making these deliveries for me three times in the past week because I'm having zero luck finding a part-time driver?" She shrugged and folded his paper for him. "Oh, I don't know. I guess it's because you haven't said anything to me about Ben Kane and about our...well..."

Her words hung in the air for a long moment before Jack said, "What? The two of you getting in some major sack-session time?"

She reached to snatch back the sticky buns.

He chuckled. "I'm just stating facts, Rei. Not passing judgment."

He was right, of course. He hadn't passed judgment. He hadn't even said anything on the subject until she, herself, had brought it up. "Why aren't you? Everyone else seems overly qualified to do so lately."

His chewing slowed. He seemed to take a long time swallowing the rest of the sticky bun then washing it down with coffee.

She, Layla and Mallory knew that Jack Daniels was a recovering alcoholic. In the beginning he had quipped that it was his destiny, having been named after hard liquor. But Reilly knew how serious the situation was. She had even attended a couple of AA meetings with him back when they'd first met three years ago. And every now and again he took up smoking to see him through the rough spots. But she realized with a start that he never really talked about that time much. In fact, he never really talked about much at all. He merely seemed to enjoy their company. Was drawn to the tightly knit group of friends that had come together after that comedic incident outside Layla's free clinic three years ago.

"I'm the last one to be judging anyone," he said quietly.

He rolled up the top of the bag and put it on the island.

"Besides, I figure you're getting enough from Layla and Mall. Lord knows I'm getting an earful."

Reilly frowned and propped her elbow on the counter then rested her head in her hand. "I don't know. I mean on the one hand I understand their concern. On the other…"

"You wish they'd just butt out."

Reilly smiled at the handsome man next to her. "That about covers it." She traced a path on the clean tile of the counter. "Tell me, Jack, how come none of us ever…well, you know, dated you? I mean, I know we three women made a pact in the beginning.

Decided that if this friendship was to work, then we would have to swear off any designs on you. But…"

Jack stared at her for a long moment. "But?"

She smiled. "You're not going to help me out on this one, are you?"

He shook his head and grinned. "Nope." He waggled a finger at her. "That's the problem with letting a sentence hang. You never know if the other person is going to pick it up for you."

Reilly reached for his coffee and took a long pull of the black liquid.

"Reilly, you know I'm here if you need anyone to talk to, don't you?"

She nodded. Yes, she did know that. Better, she knew that she could say anything to him without worrying about it getting back to Layla and Mallory. And that he would listen without reservation.

"Do you have your two-cents worth on the situation?" she found herself asking, even though she knew she was maneuvering through a potential minefield. "You know, on my dating Ben Kane?"

He rested a large hand on her shoulder and gave a squeeze. "Babe, I think you should go with whatever your heart tells you. Even if it leads you wrong—and I'm not saying it will—at least you won't ever wonder 'what if.'"

The organ in question pitched to Reilly's feet at the quietly offered advice. She leaned into the man who smelled like the outdoors in the middle of L.A. and briefly closed her eyes. Had she ever been this close to either of her two brothers? She didn't think so. And, boy, did it ever feel good to be able to count on him for some good, no-nonsense advice.

And, of course, to make her deliveries.

She reluctantly pushed away from him. "I guess you'd better make those deliveries."

Jack scanned her face, as if trying to decipher her emotional state. When she smiled and tried to blink back a veil of tears, he grinned at her. "You women are a mess, you know?"

She laughed and cried simultaneously. "I know. I don't have a clue how you put up with us."

"Because being around you guys keeps me sane. Makes me realize how bad things can really get," he teased. Then he gave her a tight, brief hug. "And because I love each and every one of you."

She blinked up at him.

"Like sisters, of course."

She laughed. "Of course."

LATER THAT NIGHT everything at Benardo's Hideaway was running like clockwork.

Well, except for the irritable chef who couldn't cook, and the still unfilled pastry chef position.

At least the electricity was back on, Ben thought. That was something.

Of course, until they figured out who had cut the line to begin with, he couldn't say with any certainty that the culprit wouldn't do it again.

Ben could also do without the negative press the

restaurant was already getting. At first his problems had been a passing mention. This morning he'd earned an entire paragraph in the *Confidential*'s food critic's corner. "Is Benardo's Hideaway beginning to slide away into the night?" was just one of the remarks worthy of note.

Ben stood just inside the kitchen door, looking through the round window at the customers beyond. Everything appeared normal enough. The diners were laughing and drinking and eating just like any other night. Except that maybe a couple more tables than usual stood empty. And that a few of the guests seemed to be looking around as if waiting for something to happen.

But it was one guest in particular who held his attention most.

"Guess who."

Warm soft hands slid to cover his eyes, making him smile wider than he had all day.

He hadn't expected Reilly. In fact, when he'd talked to her an hour or so ago, she hadn't breathed word one about making the drive out to the coast. She'd said something about finishing up an order then soaking in a hot bath and reading a good book before calling it an early night.

Ben slid his hands up her arms, awfully glad she'd either changed her mind or lied to him flat-out.

"Heidi?"

Her hands froze.

He chuckled then pulled her to his front so he could haul her to him, stiff back and all.

"That wasn't even near funny," she said, her hazel eyes shooting fireballs at him.

"So my sense of humor needs a bit of an adjustment." He grinned. "Care to help me with it?"

"No." She pushed against his chest. "Actually, you're not even the one I'm here to see."

He raised his brows, admitting to a stinging sensation in his stomach. "Oh?"

She made a face at him and he had the feeling he was going to pay for the Heidi comment. "Yes." She picked up a blue bag with bows all over it she'd put down on the floor. "I'm here to see Fabio."

"Fabio…" Ben said slowly.

He crossed his arms, watching as she moved to tap the surly, round chef on the shoulder. Fabio stopped barking midorder and turned to look at her, his face instantly softening into a smile.

Ben considered hiring Reilly on the spot if just to keep the old chef manageable.

"Oh, you should not have," the Italian born Fabio said, throwing his right arm wide and catching her in a bear hug.

"You haven't seen what's in the bag yet," Reilly objected.

Fabio gestured widely. "Does not matter. So long as it is from you, no?"

Reilly laughed and fished something out of the bag. "Here. Let me take that napkin you have tied around your shoulder," she said. She carefully replaced it with a red sling bearing white words that read That's "Boss" to You.

Ben rubbed his chin and grinned.

He watched as she pulled items out of the bag one by one. A specialized under-the-cast scratcher. A megaphone for the moments when he thought no one was listening to him and finally a collapsible chair so he might rest from time to time.

Fabio's smile was as big as the kitchen. "You, you are the most beautiful woman in the whole world, Signorina Reilly."

Ben took in her deep flush as Fabio kissed her heartily on both cheeks then turned to show off the gifts to the rest of the staff. Ben didn't miss the groans from the cooks who had been taking the brunt of Fabio's bad temper up until now, but the sounds were good-natured because Fabio appeared to have made a complete one-eighty the instant he laid eyes on Reilly.

Ben looked Reilly over from the top of her sexy head to the tips of her sandal-covered toes, knowing exactly where Fabio was coming from.

The door to the kitchen swung open and a server entered. When the door closed again, Ben stepped to it to look out.

"What's the matter?" Reilly asked, coming to stand next to him.

He said simply, "It's Monday."

"Uh-huh…at least it was the last time I checked."

He looked at her.

"Monday…Monday…oh! Monday!" She jostled him aside so she could look through the window. "Where is he?"

"Who?" he asked needlessly, slightly put out. Why did he get the impression that out of the two of them she would be the one to forget their anniversary?

"Your father, of course," she said, sliding him a stare. "Wait, wait. He's the one at the end of the bar, right?"

Ben stretched his neck then straightened his tie. "How'd you guess?"

"Because he's the one who looks like he wants to run for the door."

Ben grimaced.

"I'm just kidding, silly." She put her arm around him. "I knew it was him because the two of you look so much alike."

"We do?"

Ben looked through the window, having to put his head right next to Reilly's in order to do so.

He'd never really noticed the similarities before, but now that he looked at his old man through Reilly's eyes, he saw the resemblance. He and his father had the same straight nose. The same thick dark hair. The same tall, gangly build.

"What's his name?" she asked.

"Huh?"

"His name?" She pulled back to look at Ben. "He does have one, doesn't he?"

Ben was too busy watching his father peel the label off the bottle of beer Ben had special ordered for him. "Jerry."

Reilly began to push through the door. Ben caught her arm. "Where are you going?"

She blinked those fathomless hazel eyes at him. "To introduce myself, of course. And to keep him company. No one likes to eat alone."

Of course. Why hadn't he thought of that?

Still, Ben could do little more than play bystander as Reilly stepped out into the dining area then approached his father, a friendly smile on her face while his father merely frowned at her.

Why did he get the feeling this whole idea was going to be a disaster? That inviting his father to come to the restaurant was a mistake?

He paced slightly away from the door and stayed to the side when a server went out and another came in. He'd been open for seven years and he'd never worried about what his father thought before.

The question was, why was he so concerned now?

And just what was Reilly saying to him?

13

JERRY KANE was as handsome and charming as his son was. And Reilly was genuinely enjoying her conversation with him. Having both been born and raised in L.A., they discussed the differences between the true natives and the transplants, what it had been like for him when he'd bought his first hot-dog stand at nineteen and how she'd used her grandmother's money to start up her own company six months ago. He had stories about the fifties and sixties era screen actors that made her jaw drop, and even had a theory on the Black Dahlia murder that had gone unsolved so many years ago.

Reilly was mesmerized. By him. By his stories. And by all that he knew about Ben and she never would.

"You know," Reilly said, accepting a refill of a diet cola while the server took away Jerry's finished plate of Jerry's Gourmet Hot Dog. "Ben hardly says anything about his mother."

Jerry stared down at his beer, his expression as sober as she'd seen it since she first sat next to him. "He wouldn't. Mostly because there isn't that much to tell."

She glanced over at the kitchen door, finding Ben staring at the two of them like a young child caught outside the candy shop with no money in his pocket. She wondered why he didn't come out. Why he didn't join them.

"Ben's mother," Jerry said, staring at the wall, though she suspected he didn't see it or the many awards it held. "I met her one day when she ordered a hot dog with ketchup and no mustard." Jerry shrugged, an almost wistful smile on his face. "She was so beautiful I couldn't tell her that no self-respecting hot dog lover puts ketchup on a hot dog." He grinned at her. "But I did ask her for a date. Three weeks later we drove to Vegas and got married."

"That's romantic," Reilly said with a sigh.

He nodded. "It was. At the time. A real whirlwind romance, that one. The best and only of my life."

Reilly wanted to ask questions but felt that in this case it was better not to pry. Let him share what he would without her poking around painful scars.

He looked at her, his blue eyes a little cloudier than Ben's, but no less powerful in their ability to capture her attention. "She was a dancer, she was. Even appeared in a couple of those dance swim movies with Esther Williams." He shook his head. "I remember waking up every morning trying to figure out how I'd ever managed to land her. A real beauty."

Reilly glanced around the restaurant and the old framed movie posters hanging there. She hadn't noticed before, but near the front door hung a photo of a beautiful, leggy blonde, posing for the camera. Ben's mother? She didn't have the heart to ask considering she didn't know where the story would go.

Jerry sipped at his beer. "Almost two months to the day we got married she found out she was pregnant."

"With Ben?"

He nodded. "With Ben."

He didn't immediately offer anything more and Reilly fidgeted a bit. "That must have been a happy time for you," she asked, praying she hadn't put her entire foot in her mouth.

He glanced at her, the expression on his face one of genuine puzzlement. "Ben really hasn't said anything about his mother to you, has he?"

She shook her head, wondering where that put her on a scale of one to ten in the dating game. Minus two?

"That's all right. I don't imagine he talks to anyone about her. Lord knows the two of us never discuss her." He shook his head. "The day after Ben was born, she just up and left the hospital and never came back again."

Reilly's breath hitched in her throat.

Jerry nodded. "Yes, you heard me right. In her note, she said something about a baby not being in her plans. I already knew that she would have gotten rid of him if she could have. But abortion was illegal in those days. And I wouldn't let her go to one of those butchers." He briefly closed his eyes. "I kept thinking that if I loved her enough, if I showed enough enthusiasm for the baby, she'd come around, you know? Alter her plans to become the next big star.''

Oh, God. ''So Ben never knew his mother?''

Jerry shook his head. ''No. I never let him see the letter. Or the postcard I got from her once. From Atlantic City. She said she was working as a showgirl there. It was brief, to the point and didn't mention Ben at all. I'm not sure she even knew his name. I named him after she left. After my own father.''

Reilly's gaze was drawn back to the man standing behind the kitchen window. Her heart gave a tender squeeze. So macho. So confident.

So much like a little boy that had never known his mother and craved approval from his father.

''That must have been hard for the two of you.''

Jerry chuckled. ''Hard is a state of mind. It was our reality. And I think we made a pretty good run of it.'' He picked up his beer bottle and gestured around the restaurant. ''By the looks of it, we've made a very good run of it.''

Reilly smiled. ''Ben would probably like to hear that you approve.''

Jerry glanced at her, his face full of surprise. ''Ben? No. He's always known what he wants, and I'm sure he got it. He doesn't need my approval anymore.''

Reilly gently touched his arm. ''Oh, I think he needs it more than you know.''

BEN WAS in the way. He'd had to move to the side of the door to let servers in and out so often he was wearing a recognizable path in the tile under his feet.

What were they talking about? He noticed the way Reilly touched his father's arm and felt a burst of curiosity, and of warmth so strong it nearly knocked him off balance.

His father looked to be getting up from his stool. Ben knew a moment of panic. This was his dad's first time at his restaurant, and aside from sitting with him for five minutes when he'd first arrived, Ben had barely said two words to him.

And now his dad was leaving.

Adrenaline pushed Ben through the kitchen door where he nearly hit one of the waitresses square in the kisser.

He apologized, asked if she was all right, then headed for the bar and his father.

"Ben!" Reilly said, a huge smile lighting her pretty face.

Ben looked at his father. "Leaving so soon?"

Jerry didn't meet his gaze. "Never let it be said that a Kane overstayed his welcome." He squared his shoulders, making Ben even more aware that Reilly had been right in comparing them. "You're obviously busy. I'll only be in the way."

"Oh, you're not," Reilly said, pushing from her stool to stand next to him.

Silence stretched between the threesome until Reilly cleared her throat, throwing a stern look Ben's way. He wanted to say, "What? What did I do?" but didn't.

Instead, he listened to her say, "Well, Mr. Kane, it was a true pleasure to meet you. I hope this isn't the last time our paths cross."

His father grinned in a way Ben didn't think he'd seen him grin before. "The pleasure was all mine, Ms. Chudowski."

Ben was the recipient of another one of those stern gazes, then Reilly left the two men alone as she headed back toward the kitchen.

"Nice girl," Jerry said. "And pretty to boot."

"Yes, she is, isn't she?" Not exactly what he'd been expecting to hear. Not that he didn't appreciate his father's appreciation of Reilly, but he'd waited so long to hear what his father had to say about Benardo's Hideaway. And that's what he wanted to come out of his dad's mouth.

"Enjoy dinner?" Ben asked.

Jerry looked back at the bar that had already been wiped clean when he wasn't looking. "No self-respecting hot-dog lover puts beans on their hot dog."

Ben blinked. That was it? That was all he had to say?

Jerry clamped a hand on his shoulder. "But it was damn good, son." He squeezed almost to the point of pain, the same way he used to when Ben was a kid. The only real display of emotion that had been allowed in the Kane house. "I'm proud of you." He looked around. "This is some place you got here. A comfortable place where a man can enjoy a good beer and good company and good food.''

Ben felt like a ten-story building had just been lifted off him, no matter how hard his father continued to grip him. ''It's not a hot-dog stand.''

His father chuckled and shook his head. ''No. That it's not. But that's not necessarily a bad thing, either.''

Ben squinted at him. ''But I thought…''

His father waited. But when Ben couldn't seem to get the words out, Jerry said, ''But you thought I'd be disappointed because it wasn't one of the hot-dog stands.''

Ben nodded.

''Hell, boy, those stands nearly killed me. I was happy you sold them when you did.''

Ben didn't know what to say at first. Then he threw back his head and howled with laughter.

He gathered his father up in a giant bear hug, showing the type of emotion he was sure Jerry Kane had never experienced before with another man. And damn it felt good.

''You're a stubborn old cuss, you know that, Pops?''

He felt his father's arms make an awkward move to encircle him, then he was returning the hug fullheartedly. ''Just remember, the apple never falls far from the tree, son.''

BEN BACKED Reilly into his house and kicked the door closed with his foot as he freed his left hand from where it was welded to her firm bottom so he could turn on the lights.

"You're a miracle worker," he said, kissing her again and again, ravenously, unable to get enough of her. "You should be elevated to the status of saint."

Reilly laughed, exposing her neck to him. He took complete advantage and dove in for some major nuzzling action. "If I were a saint, would you be doing what you are?"

Ben knew a moment of pause, then he grinned against her sweet-smelling skin. "No."

"Well, then."

He worked his hand up under the hem of her skirt and made a beeline for the crotch of her panties. She gasped.

"I've got to tell you," she whispered. "You didn't make it easy on me. I swear, I thought you were going to stay in the kitchen and just watch your father leave without saying goodbye."

Ben closed his eyes and groaned, his concentration momentarily broken. "I was afraid I was, too." He nipped at her neck. "But I had to know. I had to find out what he thought."

"And?" she asked, working her hands up under his shirt.

"And he liked the place."

She caught his head in her hands. "Ben, baby, he loved it."

He was sure the grin he wore was stupid, but he couldn't help it. "Yeah, he did, didn't he?"

She laughed and planted a wet one right on his mouth. "You're incorrigible."

"And you need to get out of those clothes."

He made another dive for her panties. Was she wearing a thong? Dear Lord, she was. "These have to go," he said, grabbing the crotch and pulling. The telltale tearing made her gasp.

"What are you doing? Do you know how much those cost?"

He pulled back to see how upset she really was. Her cheeks were pink, and her eyes glistened, but within an instant she was kissing him again, all forgiven.

Oh, how he was coming to love this woman.

He maneuvered her toward his bedroom, this time not bothering to open the drapes and the windows but rather launching her straight across his bed.

She squealed in surprise as she bounced once, twice, then pushed herself up to sit.

It was all he could do not to jump on her right then. Instead he headed for the connecting bath and turned on the hot tub. He returned to find her sitting right where he'd left her, looking a bit puzzled.

"What?" she asked when he remained standing by the bed.

"Nothing. I'm just enjoying the view."

She looked down to find her skirt bunched up around her waist, baring her pink flesh to his gaze. She tugged on the hem, partially covering herself. "Perv."

"Flasher." He strode across the room away from the bed.

"What are you doing now?" she asked, obviously impatient for him to join her.

"Hold on a minute. I bought you something today."

She pushed herself up farther. "For me? You got me a gift?"

He opened a drawer and took out a red, wrapped package. "Actually, it's more for me than it is for you."

Reilly frowned after he tossed it to her. She shook the package beside her ear. "I thought the point was to get me out of my clothes, not make me put different ones on."

He dropped his trousers then shrugged out of his shirt. "Would you just open the damn gift, Rei?"

"Well, I can already tell it's not a ring box," she said.

Ben stared at her. "What?"

She made a face. "Nothing." She tore into the paper. Ben would have given a little more thought to what she'd just said except he was anxious to see her reaction to what he'd bought.

The sound she made when she stared at the box's contents was between horrified and disgusted.

"Oh, God," she muttered, holding up the pair of enormous panties with the tip of her index finger. "You can't be serious." She dropped the white cotton back into the box and closed it as if trying to contain an army of ants. "You're never going to let me live those underpants down, are you?"

He grabbed the box and took the pants back out. "Oh, no. Actually, I want you to promise me that from here on in these are the only type of underpants you'll wear."

She blinked at him as if he'd left his brain back at the restaurant. "You are a pervert, aren't you?"

"You're the one who wears them, so what does that make you?"

She tried to snatch the panties away from him. "I *used to* wear them. And I wore them because they were comfortable. Period. Not because I, even in my most ridiculous fantasies, ever thought they were sexy."

He waggled his brows at her. "That's because you're not privy to some of the dreams I've had." He curved his fingers around one of her ankles and hauled her toward the edge of the bed. "Come here and let me put these on."

She kicked at him. "You are not putting those things on me, Ben!"

"What? Aren't they the right size?"

She reached for the panties to check the tag inside. "Yes, they're the right size. Which makes me feel even worse, thank you."

Ben grinned. "Oh, don't feel bad, baby. Put these on and I'll do anything you want."

She gazed at him speechlessly for a few moments, her bottom lip disappearing between her even white teeth. "Anything?"

He grinned at her. "Uh-huh."

She heaved a sigh. "Okay." She raised a finger. "But only for a little while."

He was willing to settle for a single minute at that point he was so hot to see her with the white cotton on.

He helped her shimmy out of her skirt and blouse then motioned for her to lie back. She did so, but didn't look too happy about it. He took one foot and nibbled at the instep, then slid the leg elastic over it, then did the same with her other foot. Then with his teeth he dragged the front of the underpants up her shins, past her knees then up her thighs. If her quick intake of breath was any indication, she was enjoying his unique approach to dressing her.

Considering the throbbing of his arousal, he wasn't having a bad time, either.

He reached the springy curls at the apex of her thighs and paused. He couldn't resist burrowing his nose inside the lush forest, breathing in her musky scent, nudging her bud with the tip of his nose. Her back came up off the bed and he took full advantage, tugging up the underpants the rest of the way, then smoothing the sides up with his hands. He sat back on his heels to take in his handiwork.

Damn, maybe he was a borderline pervert. Because he was probably the only guy in the world who found these droopy, flesh-covering things exciting. The waist of the underpants stretched up to cover her tiny navel, while the legs caught her straight across the tops of her thighs.

But it really wasn't the panties he was interested in. It was what lay underneath.

He scooped Reilly up against his chest and moved toward the master bath.

She gasped and clutched onto him. "What are you doing?"

"Putting you in the hot tub," he ground out, too close to completing his fantasy to elaborate.

"In these?" she practically squeaked.

Ben's answer was dropping her into the warm, churning waters of the huge tub. She went all the way under then came up coughing, pushing her hair back from her face. He half expected her to be angry. Instead she threw back her head and laughed, bubbles playing with the pink tips of her breasts.

Ben made a low rumbling sound then followed after her, going under and coming up between her legs. She encircled his waist with her legs, putting his straining erection right where it wanted to be. He lifted to his knees and watched as her body moved up, her stomach breaking the surface, smooth, clear water sluicing over her flawless skin…and revealing where the white cotton was wet and molded against her swollen flesh.

The rumbling sound upgraded to a full out growl as he visually examined the area in question. Damn, call him crazy, but he had never seen anything as sexily erotic as the nearly transparent material cling-ing to her warm flesh. He grasped her hips, running his thumbs down over where he could clearly see her navel through the cotton, then down lower to where the material adhered to her engorged sex. With the hair beneath wet, he could easily follow the slit right down the middle of her sweet flesh. He pressed his thumbs against her swollen labia then slowly drew them open, baring the petal-like skin below the gauzy cotton.

He glanced up to find Reilly raptly watching his movements. She swallowed hard, obviously turned on by his unusual behavior. "I, um, thought you were going to do whatever I wanted?"

Ben grasped her hips more tightly. "I lied."

In the water, movement became easier. He used the opportunity to turn her over so that she was kneeling in front of him, her legs spread, the cotton clinging to her firm, rounded bottom and giving him a new perspective on the properties of wet cotton against clean, female flesh. Oh, yeah. He further molded the material down into the shallow valley of her backside, watching as the water dripped from the bottom, al-most as if it were her own hot juices flowing instead of water.

"When's the last time you had sex, Reilly?" he leaned against her back and whispered into her ear.

"What?" She was obviously confused by his question, especially since she was waiting for him to up the ante in his little game. "Last night."

He licked the dampness from her neck. "I meant before me."

Her brow lowered and he imagined she was considering her answer. He pressed his erection against the pulsing flesh between her legs. His actions yielded the desired result when her answer came out on a shivering sigh, "A long time. Years."

Ben was surprised. But he was more relieved. "I've never had unprotected sex."

She turned her head to look into his eyes.

"Condoms don't perform well in water, Reilly. Do you trust me?"

She nodded slowly, seeming to absorb the import of what he was saying.

"And birth control?" she whispered.

He wanted to ask her to face the consequences with him. But was it too soon to ask that of her? To suggest that if she got pregnant that they welcome the opportunity?

Right now being connected to Reilly without anything interfering emerged all so important to him he could have yelled out with the need of it.

"I'll withdraw," he said. "But you have to know, it's not the most effective method of birth control."

She nodded again and strained back against his erection, drawing a groan from him. "I want to feel you, Ben...."

That was all the go-ahead he needed. Lifting back

up, he pulled a thick folded towel into the water and positioned it under their knees, then repositioned her so she could hold on to the side of the tub.

He ran his right hand over the curve of her bottom, then followed her shallow crevice down to where she was so hot he thought he could burn his fingers. Then he slowly worked the elastic of the leg and peeled the wet cotton back from her sex, revealing her inflamed, perfect flesh. He fit the knob of his erection against her portal, then slid in straight to the hilt, grasping her hips tightly to hold her still as she bore down on him.

Wow...

Feeling her tight, soft muscles encircling him without the layer of latex nearly sent him soaring off into climax world right then and there. He'd never known a sensation so sweet...so phenomenal. In that one moment, he understood why so many men didn't like to wear gloves. In that one moment, he understood the significance of his taking the risk with this one woman.

Reilly.

He curved his hand around her waist then up to cup her breasts, gently kneading them, then flattened his palms against her to draw her up so that her slick back met his front. He sat back against the far wall of the hot tub, shuddering as her muscles contracted around him.

Oh, yes...

He leisurely kissed her neck, then used the weightlessness of the water to pull her up his shaft then bring her back down again. Her responsive moan made him grit his back teeth together to keep from coming. He brought her down again…and again…his fingers gripping her soft, soapy breasts, his erection diving deep into her body until he teetered on the brink. Then at the last minute he withdrew despite her moan of protest, pressing his arousal against the small of her back as the world shattered into a million brilliant pieces.

As Ben curved her body against his, holding her close, he came to know in that one moment that his fear that he was falling in love with Reilly wasn't just a fear. It was an out-and-out reality. And his full grin told him he couldn't have been happier about it.

14

REILLY WAS CONVINCED that just before dawn was one of the most beautiful times of the day. Especially today. Most notably today. She drove home from Ben's the following morning with a smile, feeling the brisk morning air from the open window blowing against her freshly showered skin. This sleepover, however, she'd insisted that Ben wake her at 4:00 a.m. And he'd been as good as his word.

Oh, he'd been as good as his word in everything he'd done so far.

She shivered remembering how he'd promised to do anything she wanted the night before if only she'd wear the underpants he'd bought for her. And, oh, how he'd given her everything she hadn't even known she'd wanted in the hours following their sexy dip in the hot tub.

Her smile widened as she remembered hanging the granny panties over his shower door as a reminder of their unusual tryst. Only Ben could pull off what he had last night and make it one of the most memorable experiences of her life.

Her muscles felt used and relaxed. Her womanhood throbbed and she could still feel the hot evidence of his need trickling out and dampening her thighs. While he'd pulled out the first time, after that…well, both of them seemed to forget that they were flying without a net and had just enjoyed the ride.

Reilly caught herself absently rubbing her neck, as she fully comprehended what they'd done and what might happen as a result.

Strangely, she didn't feel concerned or overly worried. Rather, she felt…complete somehow. And happier than she'd been in a long, long time. If she had ever felt this happy.

Last night…

Her decidedly wistful sigh filled her ears. Last night she'd connected with Ben in a way that she'd never connected with another human being before. More than just physically. At times it seemed that more than their skin was dancing together. That some sort of deeper essence, their spirits maybe, was tangling together, exploring and embracing until they seemed to become a single entity instead of two separate people.

She caught a red flashing light in her rearview mirror and pulled to the right side of the road to allow a L.A. police cruiser by. When it had passed, she accelerated again, loving the emptiness of the street, the stillness of the predawn hour.

Loving that she was in love with Ben.

She saw more flashing lights up ahead. She squinted into the darkness and into the lights, but couldn't make anything out. She hoped someone hadn't gotten into an accident. She hated the scenes of twisted metal and carnage. It reminded her too vividly that she was only human, after all.

She drew closer to the lights and her heart began to pound in her chest. She realized that the L.A. police cars weren't the only vehicles gathered. That two fire trucks sat at odd angles blocking the street just in front of...

Oh, God, they were in front of Sugar 'n' Spice.

And Sugar 'n' Spice was on fire.

Reilly drew her vehicle to a halt, her eyes unable to take everything in in one pass. From the firefighters in full turnout gear, to the police running tape to block the passage of vehicles on the road, to a black plume of smoke rising from the roof of her shop and the apartment above it, her brain tried to register what it was seeing, but somehow fell short.

She opened her vehicle door and stumbled out on rubber-band knees. This couldn't be happening. Her shop couldn't possibly be on fire.

"Ma'am," an L.A. officer said, barring her from advancing farther. "I'm afraid I'm going to have to ask you to stay here."

"The...I'm...that's my shop...my home," she whispered.

Over the roar of the fire and the hoses, the officer didn't appear to hear her and she continued to push forward.

"Ma'am..."

"You don't understand. I own this building, damn it!"

The officer blinked at her. "I understood that the owner was in the upstairs apartment."

Reilly's heart skipped a beat and her throat went dry. "What?"

"One of the neighbors reported seeing you in one of the apartment windows before the place went up."

"But that's impossible...I wasn't home. I've been away all night...."

The earth shifted beneath her feet. Who was in her house?

"A rescue team is trying to gain access right now."

Reilly pushed by him, ignoring his pleas for her to stay put. She wove through the cars and the trucks until she was standing in front of her building. Or what had once been her shop and her apartment. Bright yellow flames shot out of the broken front shop windows and from the windows upstairs, black smoke billowing out in thick waves.

This couldn't be happening...it wasn't happening.

"Aunt Reilly! Aunt Reilly, help!" She heard faintly above the roar of the flames.

Her knees threatened to give out altogether. "Efi!" she thought she shouted, but heard only a whisper. Through the smoke, she could barely make her out at the window.

Reilly stumbled forward, grabbing the arm of the nearest person, who she suspected was the fire chief. "It's my niece! My fifteen-year-old niece! She's inside! You've got to do something! You've got to get her out!"

The chief looked over her shoulder then the police officer who had tried to stop her from approaching grabbed her arm and attempted to drag her back from the scene.

"No!" she shouted, fighting him. "Efi's in there!"

"There's nothing you can do, ma'am."

She glared at him, her pulse pounding wildly. "Then you do something, God damn it! Get my niece out of there, now!"

He tightened his grip on her arm, surely bruising her, then pointed to where a ladder was being swung to one of the front, second-story windows while the full spray of two hoses was being aimed inside. "They're going in now."

Dear Lord…

Reilly had never felt the urge to pray so fervently in her life. As she stood there with the officer's hand clutching her arm, she stared unblinkingly as a firefighter hit at the broken window with an axe, knocking the rest of the glass out.

"Efi!" she cried, watching as the fifteen-year-old appeared again in the window.

The firefighter grabbed for the teen and threw a wet blanket over her back, holding her like she weighed no more than a sack of flour. The ladder swung away from the window just as an explosion sounded from inside the apartment, spitting fire through the hole her niece had just escaped from.

Reilly rushed forward, forcing the officer to release her as she sought out her niece.

"Oh God, oh God, oh God," she said over and over again as the firefighter carried Efi down then transferred her into another firefighter's arms. Reilly followed along, trying to see inside the blanket. "Efi, are you all right? Oh, baby, please, please tell me you're okay."

There was no answer as the firefighter lay the too still teen back first on a gurney and the blanket fell away. Reilly pushed past him and stared down into her niece's wide-eyed face.

"Oh, Efi!" she cried, gingerly grasping the sides of her face and trying to get her to make eye contact. "Talk to me, sweetie. Where do you hurt?"

Efi continued staring straight above her as Reilly checked her from head to toe to make sure she was all there.

"She's in shock, ma'am," the firefighter told her. "Now if you'll move back so we can—"

Efi blinked then looked straight into Reilly's eyes, sending the fear of God through her at the grief in the teen's big brown eyes. "Oh, Aunt Rei. I couldn't…"

The girl's torment was scaring Reilly. "What, Ef? You couldn't what?"

The fifteen-year-old began shaking her head back and forth, tears making tracks through the soot covering her cheeks. "Mom and I got into a really bad fight so I came over here but you weren't home and I fell asleep on the couch and— Oh, Reilly, he's gone."

Reilly resisted the urge to shake her out of her shock. "Efi, what are you talking about?"

The teen blinked at her as if the answer was obvious. "Blackie."

It finally dawned on Reilly. "Do you mean the cat?"

Her niece nodded.

Reilly's voice broke on a sob as she gathered the girl into her arms. "Oh, baby. It's all right. He probably got out. Cat's are good that way, you know? Nine lives and all that. I think…Blackie must have at least a good six or so lives left in him."

All she could think about that minute was that her niece was all right.

But lingering on the edge of her relief was the sinking knowledge that everything she had worked so hard for—her shop, her apartment, her life—was going up in smoke a few yards away…

BEN WALKED INTO the Hideaway at just after eight that morning, most of the deliveries scheduled for some time after that. He waved to Lance who was on the phone, then took the clipboard holding the outstanding invoices off of a hook near the door. The electricity was still on. Fabio was supervising the cooking staff. And outside the sun was shining brightly, the sea air smelled fresh and everything looked brighter and better than it had even the day before.

Reilly…

He had little doubt that his optimistic mood was due in large part—if not wholly—to her. Whenever she was around he somehow sensed the world would continue to turn. That everything would be all right. No, not all right. Better than all right. Everything would be damned great.

Okay, so it had really sucked waking up this morning without her next to him. But he had grinned when he'd found what she called the granny panties hanging over the shower stall door. The woman could make him grin at the strangest times. Take a hopeless situation and turn it into a triumph.

And the sex was...

Well, it was phenomenal.

And every time with her just got better and better.

The delivery truck from their seafood supplier pulled into the parking lot. Ben found the order on the clipboard and put it on top, motioning for the driver to back up. Within moments he'd verified that everything was as it should be. He'd ordered crab; he'd gotten crab. Every item down to the exact ounce was what he got.

"Boss...we've got a problem."

Ben resisted the urge to wave Lance away. He'd heard those words once too often lately. He wanted this one day to go by without hearing them. He signed off on the seafood invoice even as the beer truck pulled into the lot with the day's delivery.

"I'm sorry, but this can't wait," Lance said.

Ben squinted at him against the morning sun, noticing the lines marking Lance's younger face.

"Tina of Sugar 'n' Spice just called. There will be no deliveries today."

Ben hiked a brow. "None?"

"No, sir."

Ben scratched his forehead. Had Reilly gone back to her place and crashed this morning? But that didn't compute. Even when he'd let her sleep in last week, she'd provided mousse and frozen desserts, enough to see them through the day without too many complaints.

He got the impression that Lance wasn't done. He didn't like the looks of the other man's expression. Mercury lined his stomach, making him suddenly feel sick. "What is it, man?"

"It's just that…I mean, what I'm trying to say is…" He sighed heavily and broke eye contact. "Look, I don't know how to say this, you know, seeing as you and Reilly are so close and all, so I'll just come out and say it…there was a fire at Sugar 'n' Spice this morning."

Ben's throat closed. "Fire?"

Lance nodded.

"How bad?" And why hadn't Reilly called him? Had one of the ovens gone haywire while she was cooking this morning?

"Pretty bad, from what I understand. Tina said they won't be reopening again anytime soon."

Ben handed him the clipboard and made a run to

the office and the nearest phone. Only when he had the receiver in his hand did he realize he didn't know where to call. He only had the number for Sugar 'n' Spice. He tried it. And was told that it was out of order.

He called out to Lance. "Where can I get a hold of Tina?"

Lance shook his head. "She refused to give me a number."

Ben stared at him. "What do you mean she refused to give you one?"

"Just what I said, boss. She wouldn't give me one. Said that they'd be in contact…whenever."

Ben paced across his office several times, still palming the receiver. When the off-the-hook beeping started, he punched down the disconnect then did a *69. The announcement told him that the call back option could not be initiated during this time.

He slammed the phone down, nearly breaking the plastic in half, then he strode from the office toward the door.

"Where are you going?" Lance asked.

"To make sure Reilly's okay." And, damn it, he wasn't going to stop until he found out.

REILLY SAT next to Efi's hospital bed, staring at her niece's sleeping face, clutching her skinny hand like it might be the last time she ever touched it again. But all that kept running through her mind was that Efi was going to be fine. She'd suffered some major smoke inhalation—it terrified her to learn that the majority of fire-related deaths were due to smoke inhalation—but given a few days rest, and oxygen when she needed it, there was no reason to believe she wouldn't make a full recovery.

Reilly reached over to smooth back Efi's hair, even shorter now that it had been singed to within an inch of its life. The pink dye was all but a distant memory, leaving behind Efi's natural dark brown hue. She'd combed most of the singed areas off a little earlier, before the teen had drifted off to sleep, great racking coughs vibrating her chest and nearly sending Reilly into cardiac arrest. Efi's mother and Tina left to get breakfast shortly before Efi drifted off, promising to bring the teen back all her favorites—hospital fare was certainly living up to its bad name. The instant Reilly was alone with the girl, she'd been shocked when Efi had burst into tears over Blackie all over again.

Reilly briefly closed her eyes, wondering if she'd ever be able to cleanse her nose of the acrid scent of the fire. Erase the images etched into her retinas of Efi standing in the upstairs window, bright yellow flames lighting up the early morning dark. Forget about the destruction of something that had been so important to her.

"Jesus, are you okay?"

Reilly turned her head to watch Mallory sweep in through the hospital door, Layla and Jack following close on her heels.

Efi shifted in her sleep and Reilly put a finger to her mouth, indicating they should go outside.

The instant the door closed behind her, her friends bombarded her with questions.

"How did the fire start?"

"I don't know."

"What was Efi doing in the apartment?"

"She had a fight with her mom and fell asleep on the sofa."

"Where were you when it happened?"

Reilly fell silent.

Four hours had passed since she'd driven home from Ben's. And in that four hours, guilt had begun to gnaw away at her insides until she was afraid a touch would shatter her weakened exterior.

If she had been home, Efi would never have been there when the fire started. She would have talked to her niece then sent her home to her mother.

If she had been home, maybe she would have smelled the smoke and put out the fire before it had a chance to chew everything up in its destructive wake.

If she had been home, she wouldn't have been with Ben.

"For cripe's sake, Rei, don't tell me you were with *him?*" Mallory said, pacing a short way away then turning to focus condemning eyes on her. "I knew nothing good could come with your relationship with him."

Reilly's mouth dropped open. "What are you suggesting? That my seeing Ben is to blame for the fire?''

Mallory paced back to stand directly in front of her. ''If you weren't seeing Ben, you would have been home and none of this would have happened.''

Jack's frown seemed to burrow deep. ''And Reilly might have ended up dead,'' he offered.

Mallory and Layla stared at him.

''What? Venture into the murky 'what ifs' and 'what could have beens' and you get a variety of variables.''

Reilly felt a burst of gratitude toward the male member of their friendship circle. Jack might not talk much, didn't indulge in gossip, but when he spoke, what he said made an impact.

Still, she was afraid the damage had been done. Even if Mallory was just trying to protect her, or just needed to because of her own anger at her fear over what had happened, her words had cut deep.

Life with the captain of the football team wasn't for girls like her, as her friends kept pointing out to her. No matter how happy he made her, the end lay on the horizon somewhere.

And with her niece lying in the other room recovering from smoke inhalation, and the rest of her life lying in a shambles around her feet, maybe she was standing on the edge of that horizon right now, about to tumble over.

15

WHAT SEEMED like a month later—though Reilly was pretty sure it was only two days—she lay in the extra twin bed in Efi's room at her sister's house eyeing the bag of chocolate kisses on the nightstand. It was two o'clock in the afternoon, but there really was no reason to get up. Efi was at school. And even when she wasn't she was too busy with Greek school and her new Greek boyfriend, Kostas—who had stopped by the house to see how Efi was doing after the fire— to spend any time with her spinster aunt. Debbie was down in the kitchen again banging a few pans in an attempt, Reilly suspected, to scare her out of bed.

Her shop was gone. And everyone from the arson investigators to her insurance company was giving her a hard time. Because of the large amount of propellant—gasoline—present at the scene, and her "convenient" absence that night, as one police officer had put it, they all thought she'd torched her own place. And as long as the police suspected that, the insurance company was delaying any sort of compensation until the outcome of the investigation.

To top that off, her suppliers had managed to find her and were demanding payment in full for products already delivered, leaving her with a boatload of debt and no way to generate income to cover it.

Still…all of that combined didn't come near comparing to the empty ache in her chest that seemed to grow bigger every second she didn't hear from Ben.

She rolled over, squeezed her eyes to shut out the bright afternoon sunlight spilling in through the pink ruffled curtains, then pulled the white eyelet comforter over her head. A second later, she snaked out a hand, blindly reaching for the bag of chocolate kisses and bringing them under the covers with her. She unwrapped one and stuck the dollop of chocolate into her mouth, allowing it to dissolve slowly.

She knew that Ben was aware of what had happened. Tina had told her she'd called and told Lance that they wouldn't be making deliveries that day or any other day in the near future.

Why hadn't he called?

Another banging sound from downstairs. Then the distinct smell of something burning made her wrinkle her nose. Would she ever be able to smell burning without remembering her place going up in smoke?

With a heavy sigh, she threw back the comforter, dropped the bag of chocolates, a few kisses lighter, back onto the nightstand, then slid her feet into borrowed slippers. She grabbed the ratty old nubby robe her sister had lent her and put it on over the N'Sync nightshirt she'd ferreted out of Efi's drawer the night before. She didn't even bother checking her appearance in the picture-covered mirror as she stomped out of the room, down the stairs, then straight into the kitchen.

She was just about to open her mouth and give Debbie what for when she realized she was on the phone.

"No, she doesn't want to talk to you right now," her sister was saying. "Yes, I'll tell her."

Reilly came up behind her to see what was burning. If her sister could find a way to screw up boiling water, she would. Actually, when they were both teens, she had screwed up even that. She'd forgotten she'd left the water on for spaghetti and left the room. When she'd come back, the water had evaporated and the pan had been scorched beyond repair.

Debbie switched off the cordless telephone receiver and put it on the counter next to the stove.

Reilly made a face, unable to recognize the food in the pan. "What are you trying to make?"

Debbie nearly hit the ceiling, she jumped so high. "Reilly! My God, let a body know you've come into the room, will you? With all that's going on, the last thing we all need is for me to have a heart attack."

"You're as strong as an ox and your daughter has pink hair," she said. "You can take anything."

"She used to have pink hair. Until the fire at your shop burned it all off."

Reilly drew in a deep breath then let it out slowly. "Singed. Her hair was singed, Debbie." She backed up until the backs of her knees hit one of the chairs, then she plopped down into it. "And, trust me, I feel guilty enough that even that happened."

"You should."

"And you should have known your daughter wasn't in bed that night," Reilly shot back.

She closed her eyes and cringed, wondering where that had come from. "Sorry," she said. "I didn't mean that."

Debbie sighed and, as expected, didn't apologize for her own judgmental words.

Reilly reached out and fiddled with a lily on a flower arrangement in the middle of the table. "These are pretty."

Debbie gestured with her hand. "Gus sent them to me yesterday."

Reilly considered the size of the arrangement. "Anniversary?"

"No. He, um, just wanted to cheer me up, you know, after what happened with Efi and everything." Debbie stood with her back to her, then she switched off the stove. "Is being a good cook something you inherit? Something genetic? Tell me, because I can't figure out why I can't cook to save my life."

Reilly folded her knees to her chest and rested her feet on the edge of the chair. "Mom couldn't cook."

"No, but grandma could." Debbie sighed, stared into the pan, then dumped the entire contents into the sink and turned on the water full blast.

Reilly hugged her legs then rested her cheek against her knees, the memory of Grandma Rose filling her with bittersweet memories. She recalled long Sunday afternoons spent at her grandmother's one-bedroom house in Pomona learning how to fold meringue into cake mix to make the batter lighter. Of being taught how to melt white chocolate in a double boiler and dip tangerine pieces inside, coating the fruit and taking away its status as a health food. She'd always had such a great time at Grandma Rose's. Always felt like she was somehow home in a way she didn't feel when she was at home.

Of course, by the time she was ten she'd topped a hundred pounds. Fifteen, a hundred and sixty. And eighteen...

She sighed heavily. At eighteen her grandmother had died, leaving her a tidy amount of money. She'd dropped the weight, gone to college, then eventually decided to open Sugar 'n' Spice. She smiled absently, wondering what Gran would have thought of the shop while it was a success.

And pondering what she would have said now that it was gone.

"Who was on the phone?" Reilly absently asked her sister as she moved around the kitchen. Apparently the woman was intent on ruining another perfectly good pan.

"Huh?" Debbie's eyes looked a little too big. "Oh. Nobody."

Reilly frowned. "Sounded like an awfully specific conversation for it to have been nobody."

Debbie shrugged. "It was just one of those nasty insurance investigators. Again."

"Huh." Reilly eyed the newspaper on the kitchen table, then idly pulled it toward her. It seemed strange, somehow, that the world had kept turning. News kept being made. And insurance investigators kept calling. "What did they want?"

"To talk to you."

Reilly pulled out the entertainment section. "That's obvious. Did they want anything specific?"

Debbie turned to stare at her. "I'm not your friggin' answering service, Reilly."

Reilly raised her brows.

Debbie made a face. "Sorry. I just thought I'd make some of that tapioca pudding that Efi likes so much and…"

"It wasn't the insurance company, was it?" Reilly whispered.

Ben.

It suddenly dawned on her that the reason she hadn't heard from Ben wasn't that he hadn't called. Rather, her family just hadn't let him through to her.

Her gaze flew to the table and the flower arrangement there.

"Reilly?" Debbie said, obviously sensing something was up.

Reilly pushed from the table and reached for the cordless receiver at the same time her sister grabbed it.

"Give me that," Reilly whispered, completely prepared for an out-and-out physical tussle if the situation called for it.

Debbie grunted and handed it to her. "Fine, have it your way. Just remember, we all only want what's best for you."

How many damn times had she heard that over the past couple weeks? She swore, she was going to bean the next person who said it with the closest available object. It was all she could not to whack her sister with the phone.

Instead, she pushed the caller ID button, her heart skipping a beat when she recognized the number to the restaurant in the window. She accidentally hit it again and the number popped up again. And again.

Ben had called at least five times in the past three hours.

She felt confused…relieved…torn.

And wanted to hear his voice more than she wanted anything else in the world.

"How many times has he tried to get through since the fire?" she demanded from Debbie.

Her sister didn't answer.

"How many?"

"All right, all right! So many times that he's driving me insane."

The receiver slipped from Reilly's damp palm and landed on top of the paper. She picked it back up, revealing what it had covered. Namely a picture of her. When she'd weighed over two hundred pounds.

Reilly couldn't breathe. With shaking hands, she

picked up the paper and unfolded it. The headline read, "Owner of Destroyed Sugar 'n' Spice Known to Friends as Chubby Chuddy."

Oh, God, oh, God, oh, God.

All at once Reilly was mentally transported to grade school when the other kids used to taunt and tease her, chanting the two words she'd grown to despise.

Chubby Chuddy, Chubby Chuddy, Chubby Chuddy.

She opened the front page to read the rest of the story. Nowhere was it mentioned that she'd dropped the weight when she was eighteen. Nowhere was there another, more flattering picture. While the photo showed her months before her grandmother died— Grandma Rose had made her wear an old dress of hers and pose in front of her prized rosebushes—the story focused on the fire and the implication that she'd started the blaze.

She opened and closed the paper several times, trying to find another piece, something, anything that erased that image of her on the front one. There was nothing.

The paper rustled as she held it up to shake at her sister. "Did you give them this?"

Debbie blinked at her. "Give who, what?"

Debbie leaned forward to stare at the paper, her skin paling as she recognized the photo. She ought to, there was a copy of it hanging on her stairwell wall.

"Jesus." She met Reilly's gaze. "God, no, Rei. Why would I do something like that?"

Reilly smacked the paper back down on the table. "Oh, I don't know. For my own good, maybe?"

She pushed from the chair and stalked from the room, an image of Ben seeing the piece wiping everything else out of her mind. She stopped in the hall and collapsed against the wall, her eyes burning against her closed eyelids. She'd worked so hard to get where she had gotten. And in one fell swoop all of it was gone. Erased. Nowhere to be seen.

She was once again Chubby Chuddy, the fat girl sitting at the back of the class watching life but not really participating in it. Mooning over the captain of the football team. Or rather, mooning over the back of his head, because that's essentially all she ever saw. Getting little better than average grades because she spent so much of her time trying to disappear. To be quiet. To pretend she didn't weigh almost twice as much as the other girls in class. Biding her time until the bell rang, scribbling in her notebook when she should have been doing her homework.

All the time looking forward to Sunday when she could go see Grandma Rose, who never told her she was fat. Never asked if she was sure she should have that second helping like her mother asked her at home. Never made her feel anything but loved.

All at once she was once again that outsider who didn't fit in the world everyone else lived in.

All at once she realized her sister and her friends

were right. She and Ben didn't belong together. Namely because she didn't belong with anyone.

"Reilly?" Debbie asked from the kitchen doorway.

Reilly opened her eyes, her vision filled with the copy of the photo that hung in her sister's stairwell. She crossed to pull it from the wall, then smashed it against the plank wood floor. She glared at her sister. "I hate you."

And in that one moment, she did.

The only problem was the words only made her hate herself more.

"No, SHE'S NOT in at the moment, but I'll let her know that you called."

"Thank you," Ben said between clenched teeth.

"You're welcome. Have a happy Thanksgiving."

As soon as he heard the dial tone, Ben slammed the telephone receiver down several times, hoping to derive some satisfaction from the move but instead feeling even more frustrated. Reilly's sister Debbie, and her niece Tina, were killing him with niceness. They never told him to get lost. Never said an unkind word. But they wouldn't let him talk to Reilly and that was worse than their using every word in the obscenity book to cut him down to size.

Five days had passed since he'd gone to the shop and stared at the smoldering rubble, unable to believe that just a short time ago it had been Sugar 'n' Spice.

Five days had passed since he last saw Reilly,

kissed her delicious mouth and held her soft body close to his.

And he was an inch away from making somebody pay for that.

"Boss?" Lance said, opening the office door.

The evening crowd was already in full swung, the smell of various dishes cooking filling the room. The fact that Thanksgiving was tomorrow seemed to affect his business not at all. If anything, the place seemed more crowded. The interest was likely generated by all the negative press he'd gotten lately. And by the recent article that had connected him to Reilly.

"What?" he barked at Lance, turning over the newspaper copy that sported another extra curvy picture of Reilly.

Lance held up his hands. "Hey, don't bite my head off. I didn't do anything."

Ben took a deep breath and rubbed his hands over his face to shake off his anger. Only it didn't seem to do any good. "Sorry," he said, though even he had to admit that it didn't much sound like he was. "What is it?"

"A couple of the guests are asking for you."

Part of owning a successful restaurant was making the rounds, making the diners feel that they weren't merely customers but a part of the family. And over the years Ben had made an art out of doing just that. But for the past few days, he'd holed himself up in his office and told Lance to buzz off.

Why wouldn't Reilly talk to him? Was it because

of the photos? Sure, even he'd admit to being shocked at the first photo. He'd barely recognized her with the extra weight. And he'd taken some ribbing from the guys in the kitchen. But, hell, he didn't care if she weighed a hundred or five hundred. He loved her, damn it.

And sleeping with those granny panties rather than the real thing was really starting to grate on his nerves.

"Your publicist is one of them," Lance said, appearing to stop short of snapping his fingers in front of Ben's face.

"Fine. Tell him I'll be out in a minute."

Lance lingered a little longer, then sighed and left the room, leaving the door open after him.

He really needed to snap out of this. Needed to accept that he had done everything he could possibly do short of camping out on Reilly's sister's doorstep—and he would have done that, as well, if he hadn't been convinced that the woman would call the police on him. Needed to swallow the fact that he had absolutely no control over the situation anymore. If Reilly wanted to contact him, she knew where he was.

But Ben Kane had never been one to sit back and let things happen. He was a mover and shaker. He was a doer. And not doing anything about something that was so important to him was driving him certifiably crazy.

"That's it," he said, pushing from the chair.

Only he wasn't going out to shoot the breeze with

his guests. Instead he was going to create a breeze of his own by going over to Reilly's sister's. If Reilly didn't want to see him anymore, then she was going to have to tell him to his face, damn it.

He snatched his jacket from the back of the chair, shrugged into it, then nearly bowled over Lance who was standing just outside the door.

"I don't know when I'll be back," he barked, then headed through the suddenly silent kitchen and out the back door.

"ARE YOU SURE you should be eating that?"

Reilly bit into the end of the Snickers bar then stared defiantly at Mallory where she sat next to Layla in the front seat of her car. The twosome had stopped by Debbie's a couple of hours ago in the hopes of cheering Reilly up by taking her shopping. Tomorrow was Thanksgiving, they'd said, and she needed something to wear to her parents' house besides one of her brother-in-law's old sweat suits. Having seen more of the inside of Efi's room than she cared to admit, Reilly had reluctantly agreed to go on the outing.

And had heard nothing but "Are you sure you should buy that?" "Are you sure that's what you want to do?" "Are you sure your name is Reilly?" until the prospect of jumping out of Layla's car while it was moving was becoming more than a little appealing.

"Why are you all treating me like a child?" Reilly

snarled, wiping chocolate from the side of her mouth with the edge of the navy blue sweatshirt she had on.

Mallory stared at Layla.

"What?" Reilly all but barked.

Layla's gaze snapped to hers in the rearview mirror. "Did you ever stop to think that it's because you're acting like a child, Rei?"

She blinked. Wounding comments were much more Mallory's forte. So when the words came out of Layla's tactful mouth, they stung twice as badly.

And made Reilly have second thoughts about her own behavior.

"Ever since you met Ben, you've been acting like ten kinds of fool," Mallory chipped in.

Reilly rolled her eyes, but she did wrap up the rest of the uneaten candy bar and stick it into her pants pocket.

"And since the fire, it's only gotten worse," Layla agreed.

"Are you taking me home now?" she grumbled, crossing her arms over her chest. "Because I really don't know how much more of this cheering up I can take."

"Come on, Reilly," Mallory said, shifting so she could face her better. "Since the fire you've holed yourself up at your sister's. You spend most of your time in bed, eat half the contents of the refrigerator in the middle of the night, and snap at everybody else when you do finally make a public appearance."

"Debbie's got a big mouth."

"Yeah, well, it sounds like it runs in the family," Mallory said. She turned back around in the seat and threw her hands up in the air. "Jesus, Rei, you used to be one of the most independent women I knew. You not only started your own business, you immediately carved out a niche in the industry for yourself and were operating in the black before you reached the six-month point. Considering that more than half of new businesses tank within the first year, that's really saying something."

Reilly made a face and stared out the window at the passing L.A. lights. "What's it say now that that same business has burned to the ground, the insurance company won't pay because the police think I torched my own shop and I have a mountain of debt I don't know how I'm going to repay? Hmm...I wonder where that puts me on the business scale, Mall. In the bottom five percent?"

Layla sighed heavily. "Fatalistic. That's one word I would never have associated with you before all this, Reilly. I suppose all of us are entitled from time to time to be a little negative, especially in light of all that's happened to you lately, but...well, God, even I'm getting tired of the black cloud that seems to follow you around."

That hurt more than the other comments combined. Solely because Reilly was getting a little sick of the rain herself.

"Your sister says that you used to be like that when you were a teen," Mallory added.

Reilly flopped back against the seat and closed her eyes. "Yes, well, that's better than being a slut."

There was silence where she heard nothing but the rolling of the tires over the asphalt, then laughter erupted in the front seat. Reilly cracked her eyelids open to watch her friends enjoy her last comment. The change in climate seemed to flip a switch inside her.

She swallowed hard and said, "I don't know. Maybe you're right. Maybe I haven't been…myself lately." Or, rather, maybe she had been more the self she had left behind nine years ago.

Chubby Chuddy meet the New Reilly.

She settled into the seat, absently watching the city where she'd grown up, the city she knew like the back of her hand, roll by. Was it even remotely possible that she'd never really stopped being Chubby Chuddy? Sure, she may have shed the weight, but had she ever shed the boatload of complexes that had gone along with it? Didn't that explain why she'd always dressed as though she still carried extra weight? She was pretty certain her thoughts now had nothing to do with the pictures that were being run in nearly every paper in L.A. Instead, her…relationship with Ben, her success at the shop, then the fire had tapped into the old Reilly. While everything was running smoothly, she'd been all right. But the instant conflict and chaos entered her life, all her insecurities bubbled to the surface, crippling her emotionally and physically. For God's sake, she'd probably put on at least five pounds in the past week with her old eating habits.

She felt around for the half-eaten candy bar in her pocket then tossed it in the small bag in the car used for garbage. Mallory smiled at her, and Layla's expression was one of approval in the rearview mirror.

Reilly resisted the urge to react defensively. To fall back on that old standard of her against the world. No, while she might not agree with everything her friends and family had said and done lately, they were not the enemy.

She cleared her throat. "Can we swing by the shop? I haven't been back since the first night."

Silence, then Layla asked, "Are you sure that's a good idea?"

Reilly frowned at her. "First you tell me I'm hiding, and now that I want to face the world, you tell me it might be too soon. Make up your minds, already." She took a deep breath, battling back the words swirling in her head. "Swing by the shop. I need to see it. I need it to help me move on."

Mallory grinned at her.

"What?" Reilly asked, this time in exasperation.

Her friend shook her dark head. "Nothing. I was just going to say, 'Welcome back, Reilly.'"

16

MAYBE LAYLA and Mallory were right. She hadn't been ready to see this yet.

Layla had pulled her car up across the street from where Sugar 'n' Spice once stood. Upon seeing the razed site, Reilly had gotten out of the car and froze, staring at the empty lot that had once held all her hopes and dreams.

"It's a matter of course that they tear down destroyed structures within twenty-four hours after a serious fire," Layla said quietly next to her. "You know, to prevent the fire from reigniting."

"And for safety reasons," Mallory added, coming to stand on her other side.

Reilly started to walk toward the void. Mallory caught her arm as a car sped by, honking its horn at her.

Reilly blinked, checked for traffic and crossed.

Nothing. Nothing remained of what had been her home and her business. Not a single doorknob or metal tray. Not a part of her front sign. No evidence that a person had lived there only the week before. She knelt down and sifted her hands through the black dirt there, the smell of smoke still permeating the air, though the building the fire had claimed was long gone.

"You'll rebuild," Layla said.

"Yes," Mallory agreed. "Make it better than ever."

Reilly looked at them absently. "I don't know if I want to." She swallowed hard. "I mean, my niece almost died in this spot. I don't know if I want to stay in a place where something so horrible happened."

A couple of cars passed on the street behind them. "Reilly!"

The sound of a male voice made her heart skip a beat. Ben!

She turned toward the street, but instead of finding Ben's handsome frame striding toward her, she watched Johnnie Thunder cross the street with his ever-present army jacket and stringy hair.

"Hi, Johnnie," she said quietly, not feeling much up to small talk just then.

"Hey, man, I just wanted to tell you how, you know, sorry I am that this happened."

She nodded. "Thanks."

"I mean, one minute something's there, the next— poof! it's gone."

"Don't forget that whoever did this thought Reilly was inside," Mallory said.

Reilly stared at her friend, having completely forgotten that aspect of the situation. She shivered, though the night was warm. Had someone tried to kill her? As far-fetched as the possibility seemed, it was still a possibility. What had the police said when she'd come home to find flames licking over the building? That a neighbor had reported seeing her inside? Which neighbor?

"Were you home the night this happened, Johnnie?" she asked, scanning his homely face.

He nodded. "Oh, yeah. I watched the whole thing from my window over there."

"Did you see who did it?" Mallory asked, coming to stand closer.

Johnnie blinked at her. "No."

There was a loud meow from the alley behind the empty lot. Reilly whipped around. "Cat?" she whispered, calling him the first of the many names he'd been given.

The battle-scarred old black cat practically ran to her as she crouched down to gather him up into her arms.

"Oh, baby! Where have you been? I've been so worried about you." She scratched him behind the ears, absorbing his vibrating purr. She'd been afraid to think about what had happened to the old Tom. Couldn't add his possible awful fate to the load she'd already been carrying. But now that she held him in her arms, her relief was so complete she was dizzy with it. "Oh, Efi's going to be so happy to see you." She cuddled him to her cheek. "Of course, my sister's going to have a cow, but she'll just have to deal until I get my feet back under me and find a place for us."

She turned around, finding Johnnie looking awkward. "I guess I'll be going then."

She smiled at him. "Thanks, Johnnie. You know, for coming over to say hi."

He nodded, then turned and made his way back across the street.

Mallory frowned at the cat when he tried to nudge her hand for a pat. "That guy has always given me the creeps."

"Johnnie?" Reilly said. "He's one of my regulars. Well, he used to be one of my regulars. Some kind of Internet geek. Goes by the name of Johnnie Thunder. Not a bad guy once you get to know him."

Mallory looked at her. "And do you? Know him, I mean?"

"What are you trying to say, Mall?" Layla asked, petting the cat.

"I'm just trying to say he makes my skin crawl, that's all. The way he used to stare at you at the shop…it wasn't normal."

Reilly laughed. "Johnnie never stared at me."

Layla and Mallory shared a glance. "Yes, he did. All the time," Layla concurred.

There was a heartbeat of silence.

"Naw," Reilly said. "The guy's as harmless as a flea, isn't he, Cinder?"

The black feline seemed to give her an exasperated look.

"You forget, fleas bite," Mallory said.

"Cinder?" Layla said.

Reilly nodded. "Yes. I think that's what I'll call him. Cinder. You know, because of the fire. And it could also be short for Cindercat. You know, like—"

"Cinderella," Mallory finished then groaned. "Are we ready to get out of here?" she asked. "This whole thing is really starting to feel weird."

Reilly glanced to see Mallory gazing at the building across the street. "Yeah, let's go."

BEN EXPECTED the cops to turn down the street any moment. He'd been sitting outside Reilly's sister's house for the past hour, having driven around the block then parked after Debbie had told him Reilly wasn't there and she didn't know when she'd be back. He hadn't bought it, of course. He knew Reilly was in there somewhere, hiding from him.

The question was why.

And it was a question that had haunted him nonstop ever since the night of the fire. Not seeing her wasn't an option in his book. He'd barely slept. And he had to remind himself to eat. The thought of never seeing Reilly again...

He swallowed thickly, not about to go down that ugly road.

He shifted in the soft leather seat, thinking that while the BMW had been built with comfort in mind, long-term sitting probably wasn't what the manufacturer had designed it for.

The passenger's side door opened, startling him

into sitting upright. He watched as a teenaged girl with short hair climbed in and closed it after herself.

"Mom's an inch away from either calling the cops or sending Dad out after you, you know."

Another of Reilly's nieces? "And you would be?"

"Efi."

Ben extended his hand. "Nice to meet you, Efi. I'm Ben."

She took his hand and gave it a firm shake. "I know who you are. You're all Mom and Grandma ever talk about."

Mom and Grandma. Not Reilly.

"Where's your aunt, Efi?"

She shrugged slender shoulders. "I don't know. She left with her friends a couple of hours ago."

Ben sat back. So Debbie hadn't been lying. Reilly truly wasn't there.

"You know, you got Aunt Rei into all kinds of trouble a couple of weeks ago."

Ben grimaced. "I know. I apologized for it." He ran his hand through his hair, unsure how to deal with the teen. "How's your aunt doing?"

Another shrug. "Mom says she's doing as well as can be expected. But I think she's in bad shape."

"How so?"

"I don't know. Everything. She sleeps all day, then is up at night. She doesn't talk much and she looks awful."

Ben grinned. He couldn't imagine Reilly ever looking awful.

"I don't even know if she's showering."

Okay. Maybe she could look awful. "Have you asked her why?"

Efi looked down at her lap. "I can't really talk to her. She thinks it's all her fault that I almost died in the fire."

So this was the girl the papers had reported had been in Reilly's apartment at the time of the blaze.

"And is it her fault?" he asked quietly.

"No! Of course not." She rolled her eyes as if he was as thick as plywood. "But that doesn't stop Mom from blaming her. Or her from blaming herself." She grimaced. "Then there are the stupid police who think she did it. And the insurance company that refuses to pay on the policy until the police wrap up their investigation."

Ben absently rubbed his chin. He should be hearing all this directly from Reilly. But since she wasn't taking his calls, Efi was a good secondary source. She appeared to be the only one without an agenda. Well, one that mattered to anyone over the age of eighteen anyway.

He'd read some of what Reilly's niece was telling him in the papers. But he hadn't been able to connect the dots until the teenager had climbed into his car.

"Then there's the whole fat thing."

Ben blinked at her. "What?"

Efi fixed her dark eyes on him. "You know. The fat thing. All those fat pictures the papers keep running of her." She shook her head. "I'd die if anyone showed pictures of me looking like that."

"Why?"

She blinked, appearing to try to follow the reason for his question. "Why? Because Aunt Reilly used to be fat, that's why. And now she's not."

"And that's important because…"

She sighed gustily. "What are you? Dense? That's important because being fat in L.A. is social suicide."

"Oh? I happen to think your aunt was pretty even with a few extra pounds."

Efi stared at him for the longest time. He couldn't really make out her expression in the dark, but he could see that she was trying to pigeonhole him. "Are you serious?" she finally asked.

"As a priest on Sunday."

"God, that's serious."

He nodded. "I love your aunt, no matter what she looked or looks like."

Efi tilted her head. "My dad says the same thing about my mom."

"Smart man, your dad." He looked toward the house across the street and three doors up. "Speaking of your dad, I think I'd better be going."

Efi reached for the door handle then hesitated. "Actually, you're in luck. Aunt Reilly's friend's car just pulled up into the driveway."

Ben looked in that direction. He could make out three figures in the four-door sedan. And his throat tightened when he saw Reilly climb out of the back then take several shopping bags out of the trunk.

Then it struck him. Approaching her now wouldn't fix anything. Continuing to call her wouldn't tear down the barrier that loomed between them. Instead, he had to formulate a plan.

He absently rubbed his chin. "Even more reason to leave," he said quietly.

Efi shook her head. "You adults don't make any sense, you know?"

Ben chuckled then lightly touched her arm. "Don't tell your aunt you saw me, okay?"

"Why?"

"Because she'll wonder why I didn't say hello if you do."

"That's something I'm wondering." She climbed from the car and closed the door.

Ben watched her go then looked at his watch. He'd give the teenager five minutes before she burst with the news that she had. He started his car and backed up into a neighbor's drive before driving off in the opposite direction. It appeared he had a few things to do before seeing Reilly again. And if he was certain of one thing, it was that he would be seeing Reilly…

THREE DAYS LATER Reilly was cooking up a storm in her sister's kitchen. While her wardrobe hadn't improved much—it would take her time to replace everything and right now she was concentrating on dressier apparel—her demeanor had improved immensely. The insurance company had had a mysterious change of heart and was cooperating with her even if the police weren't and she was going to get her first emergency operating check on Monday. She'd been so relieved to hear the news she'd immediately started shopping for new locales and an apartment. She'd also taken over Debbie's kitchen.

Yes, she was definitely making a comeback.

Well, except when it came to Ben Kane.

She wildly stirred the thickening sauce on the stove to keep it from curdling. Since Efi had told her she'd seen him two nights ago, and that he'd left without saying hello, her mind had been working overtime trying to figure out what had happened.

"He realized you weren't for him, you one-time fat cow," she told herself.

She grimaced and removed the pan from the burner. While she suspected part of that might be the case, she also had to wonder about Ben's strange comments to Efi. She'd told her that he'd said he didn't care if she'd been fat or was fat, that he loved her just the way she was.

"That's why he took off like a bat out of hell once he caught a glimpse of me again," she muttered under her breath, chasing away any joy that had warmed her heart at the original thought.

She shook her head and slowly stirred egg yolks into the sauce along with butter then returned the mixture to the burner.

Her sister came in the back door carrying three grocery bags chock-full of the ingredients Reilly had sent her out to get. "It's a good thing I don't like to cook or I'd never fit all the groceries in the kitchen," Debbie said, awkwardly unloading the bags onto the table and nearly tripping over Cinder, who, it appeared, was now finally named. Efi had not only taken to the name, Reilly suspected she was going to be minus one cat when she moved into a new place.

"It's not that you don't like to cook—it's that you can't cook," Reilly corrected her.

Debbie waved her hand. "Same difference. I think after Thanksgiving everyone's glad to have you back, Rei." She moved and nearly tripped over Cinder again. "I hate that cat."

"You don't hate the cat."

Thanksgiving at her parents' house had always been a trial in good manners. Before she'd taken over the cooking duties years ago, her mother had always produced an overcooked and dried-out turkey, over salted boxed stuffing, and inedible secondary plates that left everyone grabbing for the bread and mayonnaise jar. The holiday two days before would have been a flashback to Thanksgiving hell if Reilly hadn't stepped in, sliced the turkey, whipped up two kinds of gravy to smother the meat with, made an extra-large helping of creamy garlic mashed potatoes and ladled melted cheddar cheese all over the overcooked broccoli. She'd smiled when the bread had largely gone untouched, although some used it to mop up the gravy. Every last bit of the food had disappeared, and everyone had been up for the two pumpkin pies she'd baked from scratch that morning right here in her sister's kitchen.

"What is this for?" Debbie asked, holding up a bar of Hershey's chocolate with almonds.

Reilly took it from her. "That's for me to know and you to guess about."

Debbie put her hands on her hips. "If I'm the one who's footing the bill until you get some money coming in, I have the right to know."

"So I'll go to the bank later, buy a money order— you do know I still have bank accounts, right?—and reimburse you." She waved at her with a wooden spoon. "Just don't bother the cook when she's cooking. Did you get a newspaper?"

No answer.

Reilly turned to watch her sister, who was pretending she didn't hear Reilly, unpack her bags.

"Hello?" she said, coming to stand next to her. She looked inside the bags, spotted the paper, then fought her sister for it.

Debbie sighed. "You're not going to like what you see in there."

Reilly made a face. "What could they possibly run that they haven't already?"

Unfortunately she found out. Right there, in vivid color and larger than life, was a picture of Ben with his companion du jour Heidi Klutzenhoffer.

"Oh, God." She pulled out a chair and plopped down in it.

Sure, Ben loved her just the way she was. That explained why he'd run right back into the arms of his model girlfriend.

She resisted the urge to knock her head against the kitchen table. She wondered if he made Heidi wear the granny panties then threw her into his hot tub.

"I warned you."

"Yeah, well, not strongly enough."

They heard a knock on the front door, then Mallory was striding into the kitchen looking like a woman on a mission. Even her T-shirt looked up to any task. Get Out of My Way or Risk Death, it read.

"You'll never guess what I found out?" she asked.

"That Ben's dating Heidi again?" Reilly offered.

Mallory blinked at her. "What?"

"Nothing."

Debbie was at the stove. "Should I do something here?"

"Let it all burn."

Mallory and Debbie exchanged glances. Reilly sighed then pushed from the chair. Within twenty seconds she had switched all the burners off and covered the pans sitting there.

Mallory was talking to her sister. "Do you have a computer?"

Debbie nodded. "Yes. Upstairs in Efi's room. Although I don't know when it's been touched lately, except to be dusted."

Mallory led the way out of the room. "As long as

it has Internet access, I don't care how long it's been dormant.''

Reilly thought about not following the energetic twosome. Except the only place she really wanted to go in that moment was Efi's bedroom. Specifically so she could climb back between the sheets of the guest bed and disappear for another week or so. Or until the image of Heidi Klutzenhoffer holding on to Ben's arm and looking like she belonged there went away. Which might be never.

Mallory had already booted up the computer and was doing a search on the Web by the time Reilly dragged herself to stand in front of the open bedroom door.

''You see,'' Mall was saying, ''there's one open question regarding all this fire stuff.''

Debbie was nodding. ''Namely, who started it.''

Reilly would have waved her arms if she could have moved. ''Hello? Isn't anyone concerned that my heart is breaking?''

''No,'' Mallory and Debbie said in unison.

''Great.'' Reilly crossed over to Efi's bed and sank down on it. The position gave her a clear view of the computer screen.

''Anyway, remember how I told you, Rei, that that guy Johnnie Thunder gives me the creeps? Yes, well, turns out there was a very good reason.''

She clicked on a link from the search engine then held out her hand like one of the display models on *The Price Is Right*.

Reilly squinted at the screen. ''What?'' All she saw was a Web page with a black background that was taking forever to load and the words Johnnie Thunder flashing across it. Cinder jumped into her lap and she absently patted him.

''Get that cat off the bed,'' Debbie said.

''He's not on the bed—he's on my lap.''

''Same difference.''

Reilly ignored her, watching as graphics on the Web page loaded.

Mallory sighed. ''This thing is ancient. You need an update.''

''No, I don't. No one uses it.''

''Well, it's no wonder if you have to wait so long for a Web page to download.''

Reilly shared an exasperated glance with Cinder then rolled her eyes, her heart feeling like it had doubled in weight since seeing the picture of Ben with Heidi. It beat against her ribs so hard she half expected to hear bones begin to crack. And, damn it, it was getting awfully hard not to cry. Especially since Cinder seemed to catch wind of her shaky emotional state and rubbed his head against her jaw, his purring seeming to say, ''It's going to be all right, Reilly.''

''No, it's not,'' Reilly whispered.

Mallory and Debbie looked at her.

''Did you say something?'' Mall asked.

Reilly shook her head and blinked really hard. ''No.''

Mallory turned toward Reilly's sister. "Is Ben really back with Heidi?"

Debbie slapped the newspaper, folded back to the picture, across Mall's stomach.

Mallory held it in front of her. "Slimy bastard. I knew it."

"Shut up," Reilly said evenly. "You even begin to breathe the words 'I told you so' and I hit you over the head with Efi's softball bat."

Debbie frowned. "Efi doesn't have a softball bat."

"She does now, because I bought her one. And, by the way, she's joining a team next spring."

Mallory tapped the screen. "There! Can you make that out?"

Reilly leaned forward, nearly smushing Cinder as she squinted at the Web page. Her eyes slowly began to widen. "Is that Sugar 'n' Spice?"

As part of a pictorial montage, the front of the former shop was prominently displayed—along with a picture of Reilly smiling in front of it.

"How did Johnnie get that picture? I never posed for him. I never posed for anyone."

"You didn't have to," Mallory said, clicking on another link. "The guy was a walking camera. Wait, you haven't seen anything yet."

The pages she downloaded from there, named "Johnnie's Obsession," made Reilly's skin crawl. There she was, spattered all over his Web site...along with a few shots of Ben with a red target drawn over him. If that wasn't bad enough, poems accompanied each page, and in one Johnnie spoke of "Sugar 'n' Spice might be very nice, but my soul mate won't look at me twice until I take the store from her life."

"Jesus," Debbie said, piling Reilly's thoughts into one word.

"Wait, there's more," Mall said.

Reilly held up a hand. "I don't think I can handle more."

But Mallory had already clicked on another page and up popped dozens of her fat pictures.

"How did he get those?" Reilly whispered.

Mallory hit a key and the screen went blank. "It's my guess that Johnnie was making himself at home at your apartment when you weren't there."

Which was pretty much a majority of the time because she'd been down in the shop so much.

Mallory swiveled the chair she was sitting in around and held out her cell phone. Reilly took it and immediately dialed the number for the arson investigator in charge of her case. She was put on hold.

Mallory crossed her arms over her T-shirt. "Who'd have thought that Reilly would have her own personal stalker?"

Reilly ignored her and talked her way through the events. "I can't believe this is happening. Johnnie seemed…so harmless. I mean, sure, he asked me out, but I didn't think anything of it. And I certainly didn't have any idea that he'd do…something like that."

"It's the harmless ones you have to watch out for," Mallory said.

Events and causes started to match up in Reilly's head. "All the problems Ben had at the restaurant…his chef getting mugged…the weird sounds I heard at the apartment. Johnnie showing up at the drop of a hat." She shuddered straight down to her bones. "But why switch his attentions from Ben to me?"

Debbie had remained pretty much silent until that point. "Because what he was doing to Ben wasn't scaring him off the way it should, maybe?"

"Sending the fat pictures to the press…framing me for the fire." Reilly closed her eyes, still waiting for the investigator to come on line. "When I think of all the things he could have been doing over the past six months…." Her gaze flew to Mallory. "What if he erases the site?"

Mallory held up a CD. "Already ahead of you there."

Debbie took a cocky stance. "Screw the police. I say we go see to this guy ourselves."

Reilly couldn't believe her sister was saying what she was. Thankfully she was saved from answering when the investigator finally came on the line and she told him everything they had just discovered.

Johnnie Thunder had failed to make himself a part of her life, so he'd set out to destroy it instead.

17

THE FOLLOWING Monday morning, Reilly sat with Layla and Mallory at a coffee shop/bookstore central to all four of them. The L.A. area's four major newspapers and a couple of minor ones were divided among them, but they were waiting for Jack before they would begin to scour the papers for ongoing news of Johnnie Thunder's arrest.

Mallory sipped her coffee and toyed with the sweet roll she'd bought from the chain franchise. She made a face. "These guys ain't got nothing on Sugar 'n' Spice." She brushed her hands together to rid them of crumbs. She'd hardly touched the sweet when sometimes it seemed she lived only on sweets. "When are you going to reopen the doors again, anyway? I don't know if I can stand it if you go too long."

Reilly smiled from ear to ear and produced a bag of her own sticky buns. "Just make sure you save a couple for Jack."

"No way!" Mallory said, today's T-shirt saying You Snooze, You Lose.

"You didn't answer her question," Layla pointed out.

"No, I didn't, did I?" She shrugged her shoulders. "I won't know for sure until later today, but I think I found a new location."

Layla sat up, her mouth full of sticky bun. "Really? That's great!"

"I'll only be renting in the beginning, but the owner says he might be interested in selling down the line. And if he does, then my rent money can go toward the final sale."

"Sounds fishy to me," Mallory said.

Reilly made a face. "That's because everything sounds fishy to you."

"Get him to agree to a land contract. That way you're both covered."

"I'm on top of it, Mall." She looked down at the newspapers before her. It had been two days since they'd figured out that Johnnie Thunder was behind not only the torching of Sugar 'n' Spice, but the troubles that Ben had encountered, as well. Johnnie, a thirtysomething only child of an older Hollywood couple, who lived off his trust fund, had been arrested and the district attorney's office had promised to go all the way with attempted murder charges. While there were some pretty strong stalking laws in the books, Johnnie had crossed the line into breaking the law. Efi's injuries and Johnnie's having reported seeing "Reilly" in the apartment when it caught on fire were pretty condemning.

At this point, though, Reilly was happy that the

press had shifted their attention from her and her fat pictures to Johnnie.

"I've got to look," she said, unable to wait another minute for Jack.

The instant the words were out of her mouth, all three of them attacked their papers, scanning the front pages, then opening them to the second pages and the local news sections, then finally they moved on to the entertainment section.

Chubby Chuddy...

Reilly cringed when she read the headline across the top of a photograph. Damn, she'd thought that was all over with. She dropped her gaze to see which photo they'd gotten of her now. Only the picture wasn't of her. Rather it was a grainy black-and-white shot of an overweight dark-haired guy.

"Great. Now they've turned me into a transsexual," she muttered under her breath. She really didn't know how the real celebrities handled it. The rumors. The innuendo. The out-and-out lies.

Layla gasped. "Oh, God, Reilly, read the piece for cripe's sake."

She began doing just that.

Mallory sighed. "Aloud. We have different papers, remember?"

Reilly looked around, but thankfully no one was within earshot. "Lardo Benardo Loves Chubby..."

Her voice trailed off as the words registered. Her heart pitched down to her feet then back up again.

"Give me that," Mallory said, snatching the paper

from her trembling hands. "Popular restaurateur, and celebrity in his own right, Ben Kane of Benardo's Hideaway shared a secret with this reporter over the holiday weekend. Not only did gorgeous Ben used to be a hundred pounds overweight, he confided to me over coffee and frozen cheesecake he had left over from the late and great Sugar 'n' Spice pastry shop that he's fallen madly in love with someone. Someone who's grown familiar to us over the past week. Reilly Chudowski, once known as Chubby Chuddy and now cleared of any wrongdoing in connection to the fire that destroyed her shop, Sugar 'n' Spice...."

Mallory went on, but Reilly wasn't listening anymore. At least not to her friend's words. Rather, she was concentrating on the unsteady thrum of her heart. The longing in her stomach. The need that filled her to overflowing.

"Listen to this," Layla said, having leaned in closer to Mall. "Since Ben has lately been linked closely to Danish supermodel Heidi Klutzenhoffer, I called to ask her to comment on my piece before it went to press. Her words, verbatim, were, 'Ben and I were and continue to be nothing but friends. But I suppose I'll be looking elsewhere for an escort from now on.'"

Mallory howled with laughter. "The reporter probably gave Heidi a heart attack when she shared Ben's previous weight problem."

Layla picked up the latest copy of the *L.A. Monthly*

and flipped it open. "Hmm…I wonder if this explains Jack's obvious absence."

"What?" Mallory said, craning to get a look.

Layla held the paper where she couldn't see it while Reilly tried to keep her swimming head from pulling her under.

"It's Jack's column. And guess what his topic is?" She looked over the paper at Reilly. "Lardo Benardo and Chubby Chuddy."

Mallory feigned a shudder. "God, I thought Chubby Chuddy was bad. Rei, Lardo Benardo is far worse, babe."

"Listen," Layla said. "In this la-la-land of coffee enemas and gold-plated vomit sticks, where do two one-time overweight people who both own food businesses that even the most weight-conscious L.A. angel can't resist, fit in? In this columnist's humble opinion, they don't. And they shouldn't have to either. Because what you have are two unique people who understand what it's like to be societal outcasts, and have come out of those shadows not only to survive, but thrive. With each other."

A sniffling sound made Layla stop and both she and Reilly looked at Mallory, who was balling like a baby.

"That's so sweet!"

"No, it's not. It's the truth."

The threesome turned to find that Jack had finally made it. In fact, Reilly had the funny feeling that he'd been lurking somewhere within the shop for some time, waiting for the right moment to join them.

As her throat choked off air, and her eyes burned with the tears Mallory openly shed, Reilly wasn't all that sure now was the right moment for her.

"Oh, Reilly," Mallory was saying, grabbing for her hands where they sat on the table. "I'm so so sorry for everything I said against Ben. I...I..."

Jack stared at her. "You judged him by appearances, Mall."

An earsplitting sob broke from her friend's mouth, making Reilly start blubbering and Layla look a blink away from joining them.

"Yes, I did!" Mallory admitted, for the first time looking completely unsure of herself. "Oh, Reilly, can you ever forgive me?"

Reilly tightly clutched her friend's hands. "There's nothing to forgive, Mall. You never said anything that I wasn't already thinking."

"You have my full permission to marry him."

Layla finally gave in and joined the hand-holding convention, adding a few of her own tears to the mix. "I'm so glad you two are making up. There were a couple of times when I didn't think our special friendship would survive your bickering."

The words "special friendship" sent them all back to blubbering.

Jack sighed heavily, then got up from the table. "I need a drink. Anyone else want a coffee?"

The three women ignored him, talking over one

another in an effort to share every fear, every hope, every wistful dream the past few minutes had inspired in them.

"I've got to go," Reilly said absently.

Layla and Mallory stared at her.

Reilly blinked, realizing what she'd said. "I've got to go!" she repeated.

Mallory got up and helped her put her jacket on while Layla hung her purse over her shoulder. Then they were both hugging and kissing her as if they might never see her again. As Reilly ran up to Jack and gave him a quick hug and a heartfelt thank-you then hurried for the door, she wondered if her last words weren't closer to the truth than she'd realized. Well, the old Reilly was finally gone forever.

BEN SAT going over the accounts receivable numbers then made a notation in the left-hand margin of the printout. Only it didn't look right so he used his calculator to go over the numbers again and found his original tally was short two hundred dollars. He erased the notation and wrote a fresh one, wondering if he should check the sum again.

Truth be told, he was having a hard time concentrating this morning. A full day had passed since he'd met with both the reporter from the *L.A. Confidential* and with Reilly's friend, columnist Jack Daniels, to help him in his quest to bring Reilly back into his life.

No one had known of his past. Not even he and

his father ever discussed how large he'd been as a teen. And since his path rarely, if ever, crossed anyone's he'd known back then, it had been quite some time since he'd even given his former weight a great deal of thought.

Until he'd seen the fat pictures Johnnie Thunder had sent to the tabloids.

And he also came to realize a few things about himself. The reason why he was still unmarried and drawn solely to model types before Reilly, was that he had been working out all those years of rejection and shame left over from high school. He had been evening the score, so to speak. And, he supposed, he was still regaining some of that ground when he gave the *Confidential* reporter Heidi's number and asked her to call the redhead for a comment. He could have killed himself when Heidi had called the day of the premiere to remind him of their date. With everything going on he'd forgotten to have his publicist call and offer his regrets. So, he'd gone to the premiere, with Heidi sporting a mysterious solitaire diamond ring on her ring finger, and he'd had one of the most miserable times of his life knowing that Reilly would see the pictures and be devastated.

That's why he'd derived an evil pleasure out of knowing that Heidi was probably hovering above a toilet now barfing up her orange juice, you know, to make doubly sure that just being near him wouldn't make her fat.

Ah, yes, the dreaded fat gene. He'd inherited it.

And, so it appeared, had Reilly. And that alone was enough to make those body-conscious people interested in procreating run screaming in the other direction.

He secretly hoped that every last one of the six kids he and Reilly had inherited the gene, as well. Because in his experience, some of the best people walking the earth were fat people.

First, of course, he had to convince Reilly to have those kids with him....

How would she react to the news? Of course there was always the possibility that she'd been so irreversibly scarred by her experience with obesity that she'd run away from him, herself. But if she thought that today's surprise in the newspapers was something, just wait until she saw what he had planned to run every day until she finally gave in.

He heard rapid footsteps on the tile outside his office and looked up to find the woman in question pink cheeked and out of breath....

And grinning from ear to ear.

"I got here as fast I could," she whispered.

Ben briefly closed his eyes, savoring the moment. It had been so hard to wait for her to come back to him. He'd known last week, while sitting outside with Efi in the car watching Reilly return with her friends, that while he'd been willing to push her in the beginning, in order for them to go anywhere from there Reilly would have to seek him out on her own steam. And that the way to go about getting her back couldn't be anything traditional. She would have been prepared for that. Flowers, candy, repeated phone calls and unexpected visits, she would have been able to reject.

Reilly was a special woman who needed special attention.

And he was so relieved he'd been able to give it to her that it was almost impossible to speak.

Reilly cleared her throat. ''You know, you put your entire career as a restaurateur on the line with that little stunt you pulled this morning.''

Ben pushed from his chair, filled with the urge to pull her into his arms and squeeze her within an inch of her life.

Instead he stayed put. Reilly had to come to him. Fully.

''I know,'' he said simply.

Reilly's brows briefly knit together. ''And you were willing to risk that?''

''To have you standing here in front of me for just one minute?'' He slowly nodded. ''Yes.''

''Oh, God.'' She rushed into his arms and melted against him. And for the first time since she'd disappeared from his life a week ago, he felt complete again. Whole. Like a lost limb had not only been reconnected but was in full working order.

He pressed his lips against her sweet-smelling hair, unwilling to let her go for fear that she might run from him again. ''Oh, how I've missed you Reilly Chudowski.''

He heard the click of her throat as she swallowed. "All I know is that the only time I don't obsess about everything is when I'm with you."

"So be with me. Always."

He heard her quiet laugh, her tight embrace telling him she'd missed him, too.

"Oh, how am I ever going to be able to trust you?" she whispered.

"Come to work with me here," he said.

She pulled back slightly, giving him a teasing smile. "Why? So I can watch over you?" she asked. "Being faithful isn't just about the lack of opportunity, Ben."

"You're right, it isn't. But what you will see is that I only have eyes for you."

She pressed her cheek tightly against his chest. "I hate this," she murmured. "It's not really a matter of whether I can trust you, is it? I know you haven't been fooling around. I know it with everything I am. No. This whole…trust issue is really about me. About whether or not I can trust myself to trust you."

Ben didn't have an answer for that one, so he didn't offer one.

He heard her deep swallow. "Did they really used to call you Lardo Benardo?"

He nodded, smoothing her hair back from her face and gazing deep into her eyes. "Yes, they did. And worse."

"They used to call me Chubby Chuddy."

He smiled at her, seeing the pain still there, shadowing her eyes, though he also saw her characteristic sass. ''I know.''

She hooked her finger inside his shirt between two buttons and gave a tug. ''I guess now I know the story behind your interest in my granny panties.''

Ben began laughing so hard, he was afraid she might take his reaction the wrong way. He was so relieved to find her laughing along with him that he had to lean back against the wall to prop himself up. Then he claimed her mouth with his as if trying to forever brand it with his kiss, his touch, to ruin her for anybody else but him.

Leaving her mouth briefly, he whispered, ''Promise me something, Reilly.''

''What?''

''No more secrets.'' He kissed her forehead, her temple, her nose. ''If anything's bothering you, if something scares you, come to me. Talk to me.'' He licked and nibbled her jawline. ''And promise me you'll never ever run away from me again.''

''Oh, Ben,'' she murmured, hugging him so tightly he couldn't breathe. ''I hate that it took being away from you to figure out that I never want to be without you again.''

He pulled her back to meet her gaze again. ''Promise me.''

She swallowed hard. ''I promise.''

Ben lifted her up and sat her down on his desk then pushed his office door closed with his foot. That was one promise he was going to make sure both of them were going to keep.

It was several minutes before they broke from their kiss for air. His shirt hung open, her blouse and bra were pushed up above her breasts and their breathing was so ragged that anyone standing outside the door would think they had a porno video in the tape player.

Reilly pushed her hair back from her flushed, beautiful face. "Did you mean what you said to Efi in the car last week?"

Ben searched her eyes and his memory. "Remind me."

"That you don't care if I was fat or even am fat, that you love me just the way I am?"

He grinned, running his hands up the inside of her thighs and pressing against the crotch of her jeans. "What do you think?"

She linked her hands behind his head. "I think we should go back to your place and find those granny panties."

Visit us at www.eHarlequin.com

HARLEQUIN® Blaze™

In L.A., nothing remains confidential for long...

KISS & TELL

Don't miss

Tori Carrington's

exciting new miniseries featuring four
twentysomething friends—
and the secrets they *don't* keep.

Look for:

#105—NIGHT FEVER
October 2003

#109—FLAVOR OF THE MONTH
November 2003

#113—JUST BETWEEN US...
December 2003

Available wherever Harlequin books are sold.

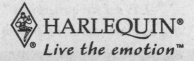

HARLEQUIN®
Live the emotion™

Visit us at www.eHarlequin.com   HBKNT

HARLEQUIN®
Temptation.

What happens when
a girl finds herself
in the *wrong* bed...
with the *right* guy?

THE WRONG BED

Find out in:

#948 TRICK ME, TREAT ME
by Leslie Kelly
October 2003

#951 ONE NAUGHTY NIGHT
by Joanne Rock
November 2003

#954 A SURE THING?
by Jacquie D'Alessandro
December 2003

Midnight mix-ups have never been so much fun!

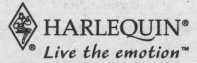

HARLEQUIN®
Live the emotion™

Visit us at www.eHarlequin.com

HTNBN

HARLEQUIN®
Temptation.

Coming to a bookstore near you...

**The True Blue Calhouns trilogy
by bestselling author Julie Kistler**

Meet Jake, a cop who plays by the rules in

#957 HOT PROSPECT
(January 2004)

Deal with Sean, rebel and police detective in

#961 CUT TO THE CHASE
(February 2004)

Fall for Noah, rookie with a yen for danger in

#965 PACKING HEAT
(March 2004)

Three sinfully sexy very arresting men...
Ladies, watch out!

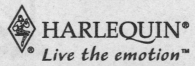

HARLEQUIN®
Live the emotion™

Visit us at www.canwetemptyou.com

HTTB

eHARLEQUIN.com

For FREE online reading, visit
www.eHarlequin.com now and enjoy:

Online Reads
Read **Daily** and **Weekly** chapters from
our Internet-exclusive stories by your
favorite authors.

Red-Hot Reads
Turn up the heat with one of our more
sensual online stories!

Interactive Novels
Cast your vote to help decide how these
stories unfold...then stay tuned!

Quick Reads
For shorter romantic reads, try our
collection of Poems, Toasts, & More!

Online Read Library
Miss one of our online reads?
Come here to catch up!

Reading Groups
Discuss, share and rave with other
community members!

For great reading online,
visit www.eHarlequin.com today!

INTONL

HARLEQUIN®

Temptation.

It's hot...and it's out of control!

**This fall, the forecast is *hot* and *steamy*!
Don't miss these bold, provocative,
ultra-sexy books!**

PURE INDULGENCE
by Janelle Denison
October 2003

BARELY BEHAVING
by Jennifer LaBrecque
November 2003

Don't miss this daring duo!

HARLEQUIN®

Live the emotion™

Visit us at www.eHarlequin.com

HTH

Single in South Beach

Nightlife on the Strip just got a little hotter!

Join author Joanne Rock as she takes you to Miami Beach and its hottest new singles playground. Club Paradise has opened for business and the women in charge are determined to succeed at all costs. So what will they do with the sexy men who show up at the club?

SEX & THE SINGLE GIRL
Harlequin Blaze #104
September 2003

GIRL'S GUIDE TO HUNTING & KISSING
Harlequin Blaze #108
October 2003

ONE NAUGHTY NIGHT
Harlequin Temptation #951
November 2003

Don't miss these red-hot stories from Joanne Rock!
Watch for the sizzling nightlife to continue in spring 2004.

Look for these books at your favorite retail outlet.

Visit us at www.eHarlequin.com

HBSSB